Praise for Else's writing:

"Else obviously has a vivid imagination and some of the story-telling passages are wonderful."
— Allen H. Peacock, Simon & Schuster

"his prose is evocative and he brings fresh sharp insight to family scenes"
— Deborah Futter, Bantam Doubleday Dell

" . . . some of your writing is beautiful. It is superb. You have tremendous talent."
— Sam Jordison, Galley Beggar Press*

"On Sunday February 23rd I suffered from insomnia and turned on the World Service in the middle of the night. I was absolutely captivated by what I heard. It was your short story 'Surviving on Mexican Shade'."
— John R Murray, John Murray Publishers

Galley Beggar Press published Ray Else's story *First Kiss* as one of their monthly shorts. This story inspired the First Kiss Mystery novels of which *Her Heart in Ruins* is the second volume.

Ray Else's short story *Surviving on Mexican Shade* was broadcast by the BBC World Service and included in the Transcontinental Review published by the Sorbonne in Paris. His unfinished work *My Father's Lies,* which includes both *First Kiss* and *Surviving on Mexican Shade*, was shortlisted for a Shakespeare & Company Novella Prize.

Cover by Asha Hossain

ELSE

Her Heart in Ruins

Else

A Novel, that is, a work of fiction.

Copyright © 2015 Ray Else

rayelse.com

DEDICATION

Dedicated to my father, who saw nothing much of interest in the
world, except when flying high above it.

HER HEART IN RUINS

The search for a lost child and the discovery of a long lost love among the Inca ruins.

Volume Two of the First Kiss Mysteries

ELSE

Part One: Discovery

ELSE

1 *Equivocados*

Fifty-eight year old FBI agent Ed Pushkin felt dizzy the first time he saw Fernanda, his suspect, from the observation room in the FBI building in Little Rock, Arkansas. He had to reach out and steady himself on the cold glass of the one way mirror. He hadn't been well, but still, something about her. He searched for the word. Luminous. She had that kind of beauty. Fernanda – Fernanda in wonderland, the thought came to him. Or was she in the real world and he a soon-to-be ghost staring in from waste-land, from the land of the used up. He watched and listened as Fernanda answered her interrogator, a young man whose back of the head annoyed Ed for some reason. Answered questions that must have seemed rude, even obscene. Her eyes went from her interrogator to the mirror, to where Ed stood, though of course she couldn't see him. She must have been checking her own reflection. Did she feel his presence? She tossed her full black hair, like a proud horse will toss her mane when she knows eyes are on her.

"Have you ever seen a more beautiful murderess?" asked the recording clerk at the table in the chair next to Ed, in the semi-darkness.

No, Ed hadn't. A curvy woman whose brown skin glowed, whose lips were full and cherry red, whose eyes drew you in, she was the kind of woman that made Ed forget how old he was. How sick he felt. "Quiet," he told the clerk, anxious to hear again the sound of her voice. Thirty-five years as an agent had given him a lie-detector ear. But more than that, he liked the sound of her speech, the lilt of her Mexican accent.

"*Equivocados*," she said. "*Estan equivocados.*"

"English," said the interrogator, adjusting his chair at the table before her.

"You are all wrong," she said, her English words less emphatic than her Spanish.

"So you had nothing to do with the mutilation of your guru in India? You just happened to walk in and see a ghost slicing him up?"

She shook her head. Her lips compressed. "Not my guru. He was a yoga teacher at the spa. It was evening. I walked the hall. His door was open, slightly. I heard a noise and pushed it. Win? I said. I saw him lying on his bed and sensed something in the room, something that whooshed by me as I came in. I don't know who or what it was. But I didn't hurt Win. I . . . I just came to his room to . . . to talk with him. And I found him like that, all bloody."

"You're not telling the whole truth," said the interrogator.

She's not, thought Ed. But she didn't cut her guru. His gut told him that.

The questions went on. Circled back around. Ed tuned them out for a bit, reflecting on his career, a career coming to an end whether he liked it or not. He felt cheated. What did he have to show, really, after a life time of chasing garbage? Of taking out the trash. What did he have to look forward to? The day when he would join his dead wife? She didn't even like him in the end, confined to her bed, unable to speak. He saw it in her eyes. She hated him because he could not save her.

Stop being so morbid, a voice in his head told him. Focus on this woman before you, on her words, on her slightest movement. Why does she keep one hand on her stomach, while she gestures with the other? Why does she look like she is hiding something, if she is so innocent?

"So what were you doing in India?" the interrogator asked again.

"I told you five times. I accompanied my husband there. He works for IBM. He had a project to do at a bank in Varanasi. He thought I would like India, so he brought me along. I did not like

India. I think I hate India."

"So you killed three men in an alley there? Because you hated the place? You drowned a man from the bank, just because you hated it there?"

She shook her head, exasperation showing in the way she raised her eyebrows and opened wide her eyes.

"Answer please," the interrogator pressed her. "In English."

"I did not. I did not hurt anyone. In India, or anywhere."

"I want to know one thing," said the interrogator.

"*Si?*"

"What did you do with their balls?"

Ed winced. The questioning had gone on long enough. Would lead nowhere. He pressed the button and spoke in the mic. "That's enough," he said. "Thank the kind woman and send her home."

2 An Invitation to Kill

Kalene tied up her horse next to Fernanda's, in front of the large glass pane of the rock shop. This was their second ride together, having met at the Hot Spring's riding club only the week before. Unbeknownst to Fernanda, Kalene had traveled far to search her out. To attach herself to her. To learn her secret, and more.

A bell chimed as they walked in together, Fernanda and Kalene. Their booted steps sounded on the wood floor.

"Chance, my ex, opened the shop about five years ago," said Fernanda.

As she walked, Kalene's eyes caught sparkles from quartz crystal clusters and nodules of fool's gold on shelves, in glass display cases, in grab buckets on the floor. "Beautiful," said Kalene. "Like Aladdin's treasure."

"Most of the crystal comes from the mine I discovered when Chance and I first came to Arkansas. When he and Randy smuggled me from Mexico."

"Smuggled you?" asked Kalene.

"Years ago. They were high school friends. Came to Mexico to get drunk. Got in trouble and I helped them so they helped me in return. I came to America in the trunk of their car."

Kalene raised an eyebrow. "So were you Chance's secret treasure or Randy's?"

A young blond appeared from the back of the store with a large toddler on her hip.

"Ah hum," she said.

"Hi Crystal. This is Crystal, Chance's wife," said Fernanda. "That's little Chip in her arms."

"Crystal?" said Kalene, offering her hand. Crystal seemed too busy wrestling the toddler behind the counter to take it. The child repeated "No, no, no" with a plainful voice.

"That's my name and my game," Crystal said, turning to face them.

"This is Kalene, a friend from the riding club."

"I saw the horses," said Crystal. "One day I'm going to learn to ride. Don't got no time now."

Kalene noticed a bit of friction coming from Crystal. Ex-wife and new wife friction, she supposed.

"Crystal watches the shop," said Fernanda. "She makes jewelry too."

Kalene looked over the pieces of wire twirls and leather strings with perfectly clear crystal points hanging on hooks. "Interesting."

"We get good business," said Crystal. "From tourists that come for the hot springs."

"Tourists like to buy souvenirs," explained Fernanda. "Chance supplies the shop most of its inventory from the mine that Randy and I part own. Randy is too busy consulting to help much with the mine, and my participation in the mine, well, that ended with my divorce from Chance."

Fernanda pointed to a picture on the wall of a handsome muscular man with thick black hair and a scar across one cheek. He held a crystal the size of a watermelon in his arms. Crooked smile, like you'd see on a homeless man, or someone insane. "Chance," whispered Fernanda.

"But now you and Randy are happily married," said Kalene, almost as a question.

Fernanda smiled. The bell rang over the door as an old couple came into the shop. Fernanda motioned to the door and Kalene followed.

"Later, Crystal."

"Yeah," said the young mother as she hefted the big-boned toddler back onto her hip and attended to her customers.

"So how did you and Randy get together?" asked Kalene.

"I fell in love with him," said Fernanda.

Kalene let that sink in as they remounted their horses, walked them on the shoulder of the asphalt, then turned onto a dirt road into the trees.

"I want to know how that feels, falling in love. I must know," said Kalene. She opened her blue eyes wide in anticipation. "How did it feel to fall in love with Randy?"

Fernanda pulled up her horse in the middle of the old logging road, under a canopy of new growth trees, a mile from the quartz mine. A squirrel dropped an acorn, right onto her horse's head, the beast quivered. The nut bounced to the road, where it rolled to a stop in the red dirt. Kalene watched as Fernanda put her hand on the horse's head and rubbed gently across the stiff hair. The horse turned. Looked at Fernanda out of one big black eye, acknowledging her touch.

Kalene wished she had such a rapport with animals. Her own house pulled at the reins, and would have bucked if not for Kalene's firm hand.

"You know, I did not fall for Randy, really, in the beginning," Fernanda said. She put her hands to her stomach, as a pregnant woman will do, cradling the fetus within. "Randy was a godsend, of course, all those years ago. He smuggled me across the Mexican border, him and Chance, when I was only 17. When I was a muchachita. But I kind of broke his heart when I left him there in Laredo and took off with Chance."

"Did you love Chance?" asked Kalene.

"No, Kalene," said Fernanda. "You are young. You will learn. One can live with someone, even love someone in time, without ever being in love with them." A rustle in the undergrowth caught their attention. A foraging mouse? "Chance offered me a new life that Randy wasn't prepared to do, then. He was too young. Too immature. Only years later would Randy return for me."

Kalene thought over Fernanda's explanation. "But you do love him, now, yes? I know you have a great love for him. I just know it." Kalene leaned forward in the saddle, feeling the sun's rays on her face through a break in the leaves overhead. Her yellow dun horse shifted uneasily. Don't you even think about it, she commanded the horse with the reins and pressure from her legs.

"Yes I love Randy more than anything in the world, Kalene. I love him so much it scares me," Fernanda confessed.

Kalene studied her face, the beautiful full face of this Mexican woman approaching thirty. She could read the hesitation in her expression. The way she pursed her large naturally red lips. Kalene willed her to continue.

"You see, I have dreams," Fernanda said finally, turning her horse. "Nightmares. Ever since India. Ever since Randy's last big project, when he took me with him to Varanasi, the oldest city in the world. A disastrous project with crazy Indian holy men. And the kidnapping. And worse."

"You mentioned a little about that in the car yesterday, going to the FBI office. All the way over in Little Rock. Before you turned up that Mexican channel. Your *cumbias*. But on the drive back to Hot Springs, you were dead quiet."

"Thanks again for going with me, Kalene," said Fernanda. "I really appreciated your company. Randy had that call from the Lima office that he couldn't miss. And I did not like the idea of going to such a place alone. I was afraid they might deport me or something."

"I know we've only been friends a short while," said Kalene, "but I could tell you needed me. I'd like to hear more about what happened though."

"During the interview? Or in India?"

"Tell me about the FBI visit," said Kalene.

"Oh, it was *casi* worse than what happened in India. You can't imagine how he made me feel. Accusing me of mutilating and murdering, not one, but several men. In India. Like I had a habit of killing! And he treated me as if I were guilty. That I would confess any minute. But I'm not. So how could I?"

Fernanda stopped her horse. She peered down, hair tumbling round the curves of her long face.

Kalene reined up next to her. Reached out from her saddle and touched Fernanda on the arm. "Of course you're not guilty. The police are such fools."

"But they're not the police, they're the FBI."

"Fools the more!" said Kalene, and laughed. She watched as Fernanda lifted her head and slowly broke into a smile.

"I told them it wasn't me, again and again. But they don't listen. How could they even think such a thing?"

Kalene shook her head.

"Why would I hurt my yoga teacher?" asked Fernanda. "He was helping me with my nightmares."

"The ones you mentioned still bother you?"

"Yes. The same. A horrible girl comes to me, in the dream," said Fernanda. "She takes my hand in a hateful grip and tells me that I am the sacrifice. That I must be sacrificed. Because I love Randy so much."

Kalene felt a glow inside. Were her cheeks reddening?

"What do you think that means," said Fernanda, "such a dream?"

"Dreams are not always easy to interpret," said Kalene. She looked away, thinking, perhaps I should tell her? Tell her that things aren't what they seem. That unseen forces are entangling us all. Perhaps Fernanda, dear one, you have been chosen by these forces, as indicated by your dream. Chosen to be sacrificed. Sacrificed because of your great love. The one demands the other. All the gods know that. The way of the world, of the universe.

A crow called, a cold breeze stirred life into dead leaves. The ears on Kalene's horse stood up. She nudged the beast forward.

"What if I told you that I know the girl in your dreams?" said Kalene, turning back in her saddle to face Fernanda.

Fernanda's thick eyebrows lifted in surprise. She laughed. "I'd say you're crazy, Kalene." She pressed her knees into her black bay's flanks; he started a slow walk. "That's why I like you. That's why I want you to come with us to Peru. This Cuzco project of Randy's will allow us to visit the Inca ruins. I don't mind accompanying Randy on his IBM consulting, but I do hate sitting in a hotel room while he works. If you came we could visit Machu Picchu together. You could entertain me with the crazy things you say."

Kalene turned forward in her saddle, aware she had Fernanda's full attention. She purposely said nothing. Willed Fernanda to want her to go along with them to Peru.

"Chance says that he's going," said Fernanda. "Randy told him there are pyrite crystal mines. They want to source product for our rock shop."

Kalene pictured Chance, that muscular, perhaps unbalanced man with his wavy black hair and scarred yet handsome face. She wondered if she should try to fall in love with him. The space between the riders grew. Kalene approached a steep turn in the road before them.

"I don't know," she called over her shoulder. "Perhaps I will." But she knew all right. That she would go. The acceptance of the invitation was pre-determined. As all things are, pre-determined, to some degree, thanks to the gods.

3 Pinning a Tail on Fernanda

Clean-cut Ed Pushkin, dressed in FBI mandated suit and tie, walked into headquarters in Oklahoma City wondering if he should kill himself. The MRI had spooked him good, the large growth inside his head, behind his right eye, had dark spiraling tendrils like a galaxy of dead stars.

He would not go back. They would want to operate, cut out a piece of his brain. His Uncle had had that done. Brain operation. Spent the rest of his miserable life in a wheelchair drooling. No, that one MRI spoke loudly enough. His death sentence. Just a question of time. How should he spend it?

He took the elevator to the 7th floor. Lucky number. Not today though. Not for Ed. The bell chimed and the doors opened half way and stopped, as if the elevator wasn't sure it wanted to release Ed into the hall in his current condition. Ed turned sideways and squeezed through the half open doors, which opened and closed, opened and closed on him.

"Damn!"

He headed down the hallway with its buffed linoleum floor. His dress shoes squeaked with each step. Faded photos of long forgotten agents stared blindly as he passed.

"She's innocent," he said, entering his boss's office without bothering to knock. "And beautiful to boot." He'd watched the entire interview from behind the one way mirror, taken by the Mexican woman's natural beauty, by the grace of her movements as she answered the questions with real shock and concerned honesty. At times he imagined he'd seen a kind of aura around her head. "If she's a mass murderer, she certainly is an angelic one."

His boss glared at him.

"What took you so long? Didn't you have an early flight this morning from Little Rock?" The man stood and opened the window behind him. "Close the door and take a seat."

"I had to swing by my doctor's office," Ed said.

"Something wrong?"

"No," replied Ed. "Everything is as it should be." He ran a hand through his thinning, salt and pepper hair.

"Great," said his boss, a large man with a spotty complexion. "And INTERPOL doesn't give a crap what you think about the woman. They sent a new missive. Want a tag on her 24 7. She is, despite your assurances, the numero uno suspect in their Jane the Ripper case." The man took another drag on his cigarette, released another plume of smoke over his shoulder towards the open window.

"Kali the Ripper," corrected Ed.

"What?"

"Kali," said Ed. "Kali the Ripper. That's what the Indian papers are calling her. Some kind of demon from Hindu mythology. She's also called the Dark One and Devourer of Time."

"Sounds like my wife and her attorney," said his boss, reaching behind and flicking his ashes outside.

Ed started to laugh but held back – he knew his boss was going through hell with everything related to the divorce. "At the university I had a professor with that same nickname," Ed said, trying to lighten the mood.

His boss coughed, acted as if he were going to put out the cigarette, changed his mind. "Well, fill me in."

"Ok," said Ed, leaning forward, motioning with his hands as he spoke. "They are an interesting couple. Her husband, Randy, works for IBM. Is one of those for hire guys, you know, a professional consultant. Works special projects around the world. That's why his wife, Fernanda, went to India, to accompany him on a project he was doing for a small bank. Did you know there is an oldest city in the world? I didn't before she mentioned it. That's where they went."

"Delhi? Bombay?" his boss said.

"Varanasi."

"Never heard of it."

"Dirty and strange, or so she described it. She abandoned her husband there as soon as she could. Went to a health spa in Rishikesh while hubby Randy finished the project in Varanasi."

"That was the site of the first crime, wasn't it? The first mutilation. Her guru at the spa? The guy that accused her of the butchery."

"No, but that's where it gets complicated," said Ed. He leaned back. Struggled to form words from the black goo overrunning his brain. "First of all, uh, first of all, the guru has taken back his accusation. I heard from INTERPOL that the guy is no longer sure who seduced him and then tried to neuter him with her teeth."

His boss choked. Sat up straight to catch his breath. "You'd think he'd remember something as impressionable as that," he said.

"Oh that's just the tip of the fuzzy iceberg," said Ed, leaning forward again. "You see, I had a long talk with INTERPOL in India yesterday before I watched the interview. Found out that mutilations and murders fitting this MO have been reported in India for hundreds of years. And no one has ever been caught. Had been a while since the last attack. Then shortly after our suspect's arrival two attacks were reported in Varanasi. The victims died with their pants down. Bled to death. Then the attack in Rishikesh days after she arrives – with her guru saying it was her, then saying it probably wasn't. And to top it off, when she returned to Varanasi she was at the riverside when two people drowned under suspicious circumstances. Two people who just happened to work at the same bank where her husband was consulting. Screwy case. The facts certainly point to her, but in this case I think the facts are wrong. I think INTERPOL wants to pin a tail on the wrong ass."

His boss shook his head. "Certainly wasn't her a hundred years ago, how old did you say she was?"

"She's twenty-nine."

"So maybe there is an age old cult behind this," pondered his boss. He twiddled with his cigarette. "And this Fernanda fell in with them? Bored housewife searching for excitement joins demonic cult? Maybe that guru in Rishikesh is actually the head of the cult?"

Ed shook his head. The darkness descending to his heart made his stomach queasy. "I, ah, the suspect struck me as her own person. Not easily swayed." He felt dizzy. Again. His head hurt. "I think tailing her is a waste. Of my time." But what else to do with the time he had left? "INTERPOL can't tie her to a single crime. They're fishing." He wanted to leave. Go home even. He stood up.

"What a remarkable modus operandi," said his boss. "Pleasure a man, then bite off his balls. Reminds me of my soon to be ex-wife."

Ed felt a ticklish wave of laughter rising inside him. He doubled over when it struck, and laughed until tears fell, all the time trying to stop. It's alright, the laughter told him. It's alright to be dying.

"They're leaving for Peru," he finally managed to spit out the words. "On another of her husband's projects. Do you really want me to follow her all the way to Peru?"

"What part of Tail Her don't you understand?" his boss said. He drew on his cigarette one last time, then flicked the dwindled white missile out the window. "Go to fricking Peru, Ed, and make sure your angelic *senora* doesn't start feasting on Peruvian balls."

4 Randy

In the study of the log house in the Arkansas woods, looking out the window on sparkling broken boulders from the quartz crystal mine he part owned with his wife Fernanda and his old pal Chance, Randy sat daydreaming. A favorite pastime, daydreaming, when he wasn't working a project for IBM. But this daydream he could never share with his wife Fernanda, though he loved her dearly and shared all other things. No, he could never share this daydream because the dream involved his ex-lover Julie. A French woman he'd met years ago then bumped into again while in India with Fernanda. Their secret affair in Varanasi had been a torrid one, while his wife studied yoga in an ashram hundreds of miles away in Rishikesh. The affair had ended, well, disastrously, when, mistaken for his wife, Julie was kidnapped to force him to rob his client's bank. He only just managed to save her. Then she had run away, refusing to return his calls, his emails. He daydreamed of their time together, walking along the holy Ganges, debating whether they should make love. He remembered the bed in his hotel, the paper thin sheets. He remembered her small hands on his bare hips, remembered the way her voice broke when she told him *"C'est toi, c'est toi.* Now, I'm coming, Now!"

After, they lay flat on their backs, in disarray, the lustful energy gone. They listened to the last bells, whistles and drumbeats from the Arti ceremony, the last of the nightly musical prayers, coming through the open window.

Randy remembered, and wondered what Julie was doing this very moment. He wondered if she was thinking of him too, thinking of him with warmth. Desire even?

The front door opened. The scent of pine and dynamite reached him. Fernanda called out, "She wants to come! I know Kalene wants to come!" The door slammed.

"Do you think that's a good idea?" asked Randy, spinning round in his office chair, feeling guilty. Never, he must never tell her about his affair with Julie.

"I think the idea is *fantastico*," she said, grabbing a coke from the refrigerator.

"You know what I mean," said Randy. "With Chance going, well, you know how he is."

"Chance is married with a baby now," said Fernanda as she passed him on the way to the bedroom.

Randy smelled a waft from her body, a potent mix of horse sweat and perfume. Of longing and repulsion. He wondered why his nose was so sensitive today.

"I'm going to take a shower. Think what you want for dinner."

What do I want for dinner, thought Randy. The last meal he had with Julie in India, before everything blew apart, came to mind. "I'm not hungry right now," he called down the hall.

"Well think on it. Maybe something simple? *Arroz con pollo?*" The shower came on. Randy envisioned the drops hitting Fernanda's wonderfully full breasts, making the curve down her sides and over her naked hips.

He found himself standing in the bathroom, peeping past the shower curtain. He reached and cupped one of her wet breasts. She jumped.

"Your breasts look huge," he told her. He pinched a nipple.

"Get out of here!" she yelled at him. "I must smell like a horse!"

"I'll soap you," he proposed.

"Out! Out!" She pushed away his hand.

He watched her then. Watched how she meticulously cleaned herself with her *estropajo*.

"We could go out to eat," he suggested. "That way, you don't have to make anything."

"Can she come with us, Randy? Can Kalene come?" She reached down and scrubbed her legs with the soaped-up sponge. "I want this trip to be so different from India."

"That's why I jumped at it," he told her, though that wasn't true. The customer had requested him specifically. Urgently. Offered IBM full hourly wage, no discount, if only he could start Monday. "They speak Spanish in Peru. And Cuzco I've been told is a delightful city. Nestled in a valley near the Andes. You'll love it. And of course Kalene can come with us, if she pays her own way."

"She knows that," said Fernanda, stepping out of the shower, wrapping herself in a floor-length towel. The white of the towel made her skin look darker. She tossed her long black hair, wetting him with a few drops. He wiped the drops and told himself that he would make love with her that night, after dinner, under white sheets, and he would stop thinking about Julie. He must stop thinking about Julie.

5 Only Days to Live?

"Only days to live," FBI agent Ed Pushkin told himself as he sat watching his 32 inch screen. The TV might as well have been blank. He wasn't paying attention. He was waiting for the pain killers to kick in. "You don't know that!" he told himself, playing the part of his wife, dead four years now. "You should let them open you up, to be sure."

"Screw that!" he said. "I told you, they aren't going to cut up my brain. Leave me a vegetable."

He knew it was crazy to talk to himself, but he found it helpful, at times, to speak out the internal dialogue. The infernal dialogue.

"I don't mind to spend my last days in Peru. I kind of like that Fernanda. Quite a filly."

"She's too young for you, she's married, and for Christ's sake she's a serial killer!"

"I kind of like her anyway. In a fatherly way. I don't mind to watch over her until I can't, anymore. Watch over. Anything."

"I've told you to stop being so maudlin."

"My head hurts."

"It's supposed to. You're dying."

"So you admit it?"

"Go to Peru. You like Peru. You've been before. Wonderful place to bird watch."

"Yes I can't just sit here and, you know. I should go, do my job. That's all I have left, really. That's who I am. Mr FBI man."

"But undercover?"

"Under covers."

"What do you want for dinner?"

"I don't know. Something simple."

Ed got up to scour the cupboards for something edible. He'd call HQ's travel department after dinner and get on the same flight, and into the same hotel as the suspect, his Fernanda in wonderland. He'd do his duty.

6 The Birdwatcher

Though flying frightened her, Fernanda managed to sleep more than half the long flight to Lima thanks to her valerian root pills. She was a fan of natural medicine and would not take the "real" sedatives Randy bought for her at Walgreens. He told her she was a superstitious child. That modern medicine was better, but she would have none of it.

She was first introduced to natural healing while traveling as a child trumpet player with her father and his band from Nuevo Laredo to Ciudad Victoria, to Mexico City and all the way to Cancun, to play in clubs and at parks and parties. When she or one of the band members got sick, they would never go see a doctor. Instead they would visit a healer. That was all her father could afford for them, a back alley healer who chanted and brewed tea and pressed rough hands on the sick one's bare sweating chest in a smoke-filled room. Fernanda loved the dark mystery in the mumbled incantations, the calling to the good spirits to chase away the bad. She dreamed of becoming a healer herself, one day, of reaching to the other side, where spirits reside. But the only other side she had reached was the other side of the Mexican border, when Randy and Chance smuggled her across. When she was seventeen.

They departed the flight together, Fernanda, Randy, Chance and a disheveled Kalene, who looked like she hadn't slept a wink.

"You should have taken some of my pills," said Fernanda.

"I like to watch the movies," said Kalene. "I love to lose myself in make-believe."

They had several hours to kill before their Cuzco flight, so they gathered their luggage and settled in a coffee bar in the airport, looking a bit like immigrants with their bags piled around them.

"Going on to Cuzco?" asked an older, medium-built American man with salt and pepper hair and a bit of a pot belly. He wore a Hawaiian shirt and beige pants with multiple pockets. He put his bag down and sat at the small round table next to them. Drew out a pocket book about Peruvian bird watching but did not open it.

Fernanda thought he looked like a serious, nervous type. Not one to start up a conversation with strangers. Maybe he was lonely, traveling on his own in a foreign country. Maybe he was trying to break out of his shell.

"Yes," she replied, giving him a welcome smile. "How did you know?"

"Oh Cuzco is a great stepping off place," he said. "To the ruins, to great hikes in the Andes. To exploring the Amazon."

"And you?" she asked.

"Yes, Cuzco is where I am headed. I love Cuzco. On my last trip I visited the jungle. Saw thousands of macaws and parrots at the great salt lick on the banks of the Rio Piedras. This time I want to spend more time in the Andes. Visiting the ruins and such."

"Us too," said Fernanda, only to realize there wasn't much "us" at the table to introduce. Randy was crossing the hall to the restroom, Chance had his head on his arms and his eyes closed, while Kalene was over at the counter ordering coffee.

"I want to hike to Machu Picchu," said Fernanda. "To experience the Inca Trail."

"You might think again on that idea," said the man, scratching the light beard sprouting on his strong chin. His eyes were bloodshot. His voice hoarse. "The Inca Trail is a serious mountain hike. By the way, I'm Ed. Retired private eye." He reached out his large hand.

"*Híjole*," said Fernanda. "I've never met a private eye before."

"Well now you have," said Ed. He seemed to want to talk, so

Fernanda let him. He talked about his career a bit, and then about his dead wife. "She was twelve years older than me. Got early Alzheimer's."

"*Pobrecita*," said Fernanda. "I'm sorry."

"When I couldn't trust her home alone, I tried a day nurse. But she chased them all off, one after the other. Finally I had to put her in a rest home. Hideous place, full of dying folk leaning this way and that in their wheelchairs, drugged up, falling out of their beds. The disease stripped away my dear wife's persona, one memory at a time. Then one body function at a time. Made her barely human. Then it took that away too. Her humanity. Her eyes, in a head that could barely move, reminded me of those of a cornered animal. This was near the end. When she couldn't speak or swallow anymore. When I doubt she even knew who I was. She'd lift herself up in bed a smidgen, then fall back on the pillow, lift herself up a smidgen, then fall back. Like her spirit, that small spring keeping her alive, knew that if she did get out of bed then all was lost."

The others had come back to the table by now, and all, except a snoring Chance, listened intently, transfixed by Ed's story.

"All *was* lost," he said, looking at the table top, rubbing his palm across the plastic surface. "I told her to die. That it was alright. That she could leave. That she *should* leave. That she had lived a good life. I doubt she understood. Whatever there was left of her. Nothing I could do. Days passed. Her face thinned, her skull appeared to shrink. Her body slowly curled up on the white linens, drying up. Like an earthworm washed onto a sidewalk. Only the week before she would jump a bit when I touched her. Now, no reaction. As I sat by her bed and watched the long pauses between each breath, as I heard the dry rasping of each exhale, I imagined inside her a tiny linchpin of a spirit sparking her heart, filling and emptying her lungs. A thing that lived on inside her otherwise empty body, a thing that did not know how to stop. Did not know where else to go. Did not know what else to do. Finally, thankfully, God reached in and pulled the pin."

7 Change of Plans

The Peruvian city of Cuzco clings to the floor of this corner of the Sacred Valley like a giant starfish, its tan colored V-shaped arms tucked in the crevices of the green mountain slopes. At the heart, at the beaked mouth of this sprawling beautiful city, lay the *Plaza de Armas*, with its green lawn and red stone cathedral, with its vortex of constantly circling traffic, wandering tourists and tweeting traffic cops.

Blue-rimmed storm clouds roiled above the red, dour Spanish cathedral built 500 years ago atop ancient Inca temples. A flood threatened. Randy thought of Fernanda and Chance and Kalene back at the hotel, eating brunch. Their planned sightseeing trip might be cut short with the storm. "Can't control the weather," he said aloud as he climbed the steps to the Banco de Credito del Peru. The copper plaque on the outside of the building said 1889.

The thought thrilled Randy, that such a venerable institution would want his help.

The woman at the desk, whose eyes were magnified by the horned-rim glasses she wore, asked him if he had an appointment. He gave her the name of the manager. She called on the phone as Randy signed himself in. Randy was escorted to the manager's office by a round-faced office boy in shorts. Randy followed the boy up a flight of stairs that overlooked the splendid lobby. At the end of the hall stood a heavy wood door. The boy knocked. A deep voice said to enter. The office was furnished in dark woods, the desk, the chairs, the walls. A dual pane window, whose lush curtains were drawn, let in the scenic green of mountain slope and roiling sky. The office had a solid feel to it, as did the thin dark-haired man in black suit coming forward to greet Randy.

"I'm Pani," the man said, offering his hand. Randy heard the door click behind him.

"Randy from IBM."

"Please sit."

Randy sat while Pani, the bank manager, paced before him.

"I can't express how glad I am you were available to come so quickly to my request," he said, his eyes reflecting his heart-felt statement.

"IBM aims to please," said Randy, crossing his legs and putting a hand on his knee.

"Is it true that on your last project for IBM, in India, you stopped a bank robbery while saving your wife from kidnappers while holding your breath in a river of death?"

Alarm bells went off in Randy's head. "Whoa," he said. "Slow down there, partner. Where did you hear all that?"

Pani stopped short. "From an IBM consultant working at the Lima office. Is it true?"

Oh man, thought Randy, the word is out. "Well, yes," he told manager Pani. "I suppose what you say is true. Though I wouldn't have expressed it exactly that way."

"Excellent," said Pani, his eyes watering. He took out a handkerchief and dabbed the corners of his eyes. "You see, Randy, I didn't tell the whole truth to IBM when I requested your services. In matter of fact, I outright lied. I don't need you to program for me. No. I have programmers aplenty. What I need from you, if you could find it in your heart, what I need is for you to find my little boy."

The words stunned Randy. His eyes went to the window where storm clouds threatened but no rain fell. India. India what have you done to me and my career?

"His name is Daniel. My son. He's only six. Just over two weeks ago he disappeared on a field trip to the ruins. The police have been no help. Private detective I hired has been no help. They say most likely the Shining Path guerrillas took him. But if so, wouldn't they ransom him? There's been no call, no note. I think someone took him, yes, but not the Shining Path." Pani went on then, into more detail, about tribes in the mountains who come to the city to steal children. Finally Randy put up his hand to stop him.

He slowly rose to his feet. "I'm sorry," Randy said. "I'm a programmer. Not a detective. I can't help you."

The man's face fell. "But . . ."

"No," said Randy. He turned his back to the man who'd lost his son. The man who'd heard some story about Randy then lied to IBM to bring him all the way to Peru. To this office. For nothing. "I'm not who you think I am. I'm sorry." He opened the heavy door and closed it behind him.

After the interview, a dejected, jetlagged Randy listened to the click of his shoes on the stone walk leading from the Plaza de Armas. "Rain already!" he yelled at the sky, but the sky did not listen.

A young man holding a portfolio of original artwork, frightened at first by Randy's outburst, held out his primitive paintings of mountains and ruins. "One sole. Only one!" the boy said. Randy ignored him.

Randy reached the turn to the hotel where the gang was staying, only to be stuck. For an indigenous woman dressed in a rainbow of colors, with a curious bowler hat perched atop her head, sat in his way, on the sidewalk, holding a baby llama. A stylish

European girl, camera in hand, towered over the round-faced, traditionally dressed woman.

"You decide how much," the Inca woman said, smiling up at the girl, eyeing the camera and the newly purchased alpaca wool scarf around the girl's neck. Randy stepped between the two of them, ruining the picture, and tight-roped the tiny sidewalk on the narrow street heading to the San Blas neighborhood on the hill.

"Yellow!" he heard Fernanda's voice call out from the hotel's restaurant-bar balcony.

He waved to her, quickly looking down as the brilliant sun decided at that moment to reappear. The high altitude sun counterbalanced nicely the chilly mountain breeze on the streets of Cuzco, but Randy knew his face would burn if he didn't stay to the shade when he could. He huffed his way through the lobby and up the stairs to a table on the balcony with Fernanda's friend Kalene and his pal Chance and that older gent from the Lima airport. The one with the depressing story about his wife who turned into a worm. The whole hour flight from Lima to Cuzco the guy had gone on and on about birdwatching. Did we know there were 90 different types of hummingbirds in the jungles of Peru?

Didn't know and didn't care. What was his name again, Randy thought as he reached out to shake his hand. Red something?

"Ed is introducing us to chicha," Fernanda said.

"Beer made from corn," said Ed. "The Incas recruited only the most beautiful girls in the empire to tongue their spit into the mashed corn to help the mix to ferment."

"We're drinking spit beer," said Chance, raising his glass. Kalene touched her's to his and they both drank down.

"Oh they don't make it that way anymore," said Ed, the walking talking encyclopedia. "Except, perhaps, in isolated villages high in the Andes. They still do many things the old way up there."

"Have a taste," said Fernanda. Randy practically knocked the glass from her hand. Apologized then, as he sat down.

"What's the matter?" said Fernanda, reaching towards him.

"This whole trip is a bust," replied Randy. He waved the girl over. "Bring me one of those pisco sours, please."

"What's up?" asked Chance, putting his glass down, brushing his arm against Kalene's as he did so.

"You won't believe what happened at the meeting," said Randy. "I get in his office expecting to go over the usual preliminaries to tie down the hot spot deliverables, but all he wants to do is talk about what happened in India."

"*Que?*" said Fernanda, frowning. "What has India to do with Peru?"

"That's what I was wondering," said Randy. "He says - Is it

true? Is it true that on your India project, he speaks real good English, is it true that you stopped a bank robbery and saved your wife from kidnappers. All the while holding your breath?"

"Superman?" asked Ed.

"How would he know about any of that?" asked Chance. "I don't even know the full story. And I thought it wasn't Fernanda you saved, but the other way around."

"She didn't save me," said Randy, turning quickly to her. "But of course every day she saves me from being terribly alone."

Fernanda scoffed. "He saved what's her name," she said. "Some old colleague of his who happened to be in Varanasi for a festival. Or so she said."

"Julie," said Randy, and wished he hadn't. He steered the talk back to the problem at hand. "The BCP bank manager, Pani is his name, he told me he heard all about me, the consulting "superman", if you wish, from a Peruvian IBM employee. Apparently my fame has spread far and wide with IBM customers."

Chance laughed. Kalene turned her head to the side with a questioning look on her face, as if re-evaluating Randy.

"I think I see where this is headed," said Ed, stroking his two day stubble. "He wants you to do something other than what IBM signed you up for."

"On the nose," said Randy. "And that is where the story gets kind of sad. He told me that the real reason he hired me through IBM is to find his 6 year old son. His son's gone missing."

Fernanda sat straight up, placed both hands on her stomach.

Chance squinted. Randy knew that was something he did when he feigned interest. He probably wasn't listening to half of what Randy was saying.

"How long ago did the boy disappear?" asked Ed, leaning forward.

"Going on three weeks."

"Lost or kidnapped?"

"Pani is sure he has been kidnapped."

"A note? A call?"

"No nothing."

"What do the police say?" said Ed. "Surely he went to the police."

Randy nodded. "He told me he has been to the Cuzco municipal police, the federal police, even the tourist police. But without a note or a call, the police say it is hopeless. They told him that probably the Shining Path communists stole him."

"A six year old?" said Ed. "And not ransom him? I don't buy

that."

"Neither does Pani," said Randy. "He told me there have been rumors. For years. Boys and girls disappearing from well-to-do homes. He just never thought it would happen to him. To his own son. So now he and his wife are grasping at anything. Contracting me under false pretenses was maybe their last gasp. He wants me to use my computer skills, and the courage I demonstrated in India, to rescue his son. To bring him home."

"That's so sad," said Fernanda. "*Me siento triste.*"

"So what did you tell him?" said Ed.

"I told him the truth. That I couldn't help."

Randy felt awful repeating those words. Like a confession of guilt. But honestly, he knew there was nothing any of them could do, nothing to do but go home.

Then Ed stood, awkwardly, knocking over his chair. He pressed his hands onto his eyes, pressed hard. As if he were in pain. Everyone watched. Waited for Ed.

He spoke with difficulty, but with authority. "I can help you, Randy. I can help you find him," he said, gathering up his chair and sitting back down. "I, I used to be sort of a detective. I still have connections." He looked meekly around the table. "Maybe, maybe, working together, we can find the boy."

"No, no," said Randy, kicking back. "You can't help. Because I'm not going to help. For pete's sake, Fernanda, tell him I'm terrible at finding things. Tell him."

"If it was your own *hijo?*" asked Fernanda.

Randy shook his head. "I don't have a son," he said.

"What if it was my son Chip?" said Chance.

"It's not your son. He's safe at home with Crystal. Look, you all don't understand. I could get fired going off on such a fool's errand. I'm a programmer. I'm paid to code, that's all."

"You did more than code in India," said Fernanda, bearing down on him with those large brown eyes. "I say we help Mr Pani find his baby."

"I'm in," said Kalene.

Chance slammed his fist on the table, smiling at Kalene. "Me too."

Randy threw up his hands.

"You go right back there, dear" said Fernanda, "and you tell that man that you will do all you can to find his son. As if he were your own. *Tu proprio hijo.*"

"You are *loca*," said Randy. "You are all crazy."

"Save him," said Kalene, "save him like you saved your loved one in India."

"But I didn't . . ." started Randy, stopping to give Kalene a quick questioning look. No, she couldn't know. Focus. Focus on the present. He knew they all meant well. But this didn't make sense. This was a police matter. But then again, what had the police been able to do? "OK, sure," he said, downing his pisco sour. "Let me drink a mug of spitty Inca chicha. Then I'll go back and tell Pani I'll look for his little boy."

"Yes!" shouted Fernanda.

"Good," said Ed, rubbing his right eye. He motioned to the waitress. "A round of chicha. Then we have work to do."

8 The case of the missing boy

Ed downed his third chicha beer. He felt euphoric. Good beer. Good surroundings. Good, if suspect, company. And a final case for him worthy of his talents. The case of the missing boy.

It could be awkward, working undercover as he was, keeping secret tabs on Fernanda, as he worked this new case. He hoped he wouldn't have to reveal to the gang, to tell Fernanda or Randy or Chance or Kalene, his real identity. That he was FBI, working undercover, keeping a tail on Fernanda. He hoped that wouldn't be necessary. From past experience he knew that people did not like being lied to. Especially by the police.

"Randy, go now and ask this bank manager with the missing son . . ."

"Pani. His name is Pani."

"Ask Pani his son's name."

"He told me already. Daniel. His son's name is Daniel."

"Great," said Ed. "Ask Pani exactly where Daniel was when last seen. What he was wearing. Get pictures for us."

"Sure," said Randy, who started to leave.

"Wait!" said Ed.

"Wait!" said Fernanda, ferociously. "He's not finished giving you instructions."

"You know I am probably going to get fired for this," he told Fernanda. "If IBM finds out."

"A boy," said Fernanda. "A six year old boy. He's worth more than any job."

"It's not a job, it's a career."

"Cheer up," said Chance. "You can always work with me at the mine."

"I want to hear more about that mine," said Kalene.

"Can I please continue?" said Ed.

Polite silence.

"OK, Randy. I want you to ask Pani if he has any enemies. Ask him has he noticed anyone suspicious hanging around. Ask him too about the Shining Path angle. And finally, ask him if he realizes his son could already be dead. Now go."

Randy frowned, turned, walked slowly then faster away.

They remained quiet for a while, at the table, on the balcony, watching Randy below as he made his way down the narrow stone sidewalk, a dark figure in the brilliant sunlight, heading towards the lively *Plaza de Armas*.

"He's not dead," said Kalene.

More silence.

"What do you want me to do?" asked Fernanda.

"I want you to pair with Kalene," Ed told her. "Use your Spanish to question all those Inca women squatting on the sidewalks with their llamas and their babies. You'll take with you the picture Randy gets, of the boy. Show it to all of them. Ask have they ever seen the child. That he is missing. Ask do they know anything about missing Cuzco children."

Fernanda nodded, the serious expression on her face showing her sincerity. Ed found it so hard to imagine that she was a mass murderer. Why he'd sooner imagine young, innocent Kalene as the killer.

"And me?" asked Chance. "Do you want me to ply my charms on anyone?"

"No," said Ed, and he couldn't help but laugh. He really was feeling better. "Obviously you are a strong man, Chance." He was a good six feet two, with a barrel chest, thick arms, and an intimidating look about him due to the white scar on his otherwise suntanned face.

"The quartz crystal mine made him huge," said Fernanda. "He was a stick when I first met him, before he took up a shovel."

Chance narrowed his eyes at her. "Ah, you've seen my muscle more than a few times." He winked.

"Oh please, Chance," said Fernanda. "Married, remember," she said pointing to herself. "Married, with son," she said, pointing at his wide chest.

Ed stood. Touched his forehead. A sudden breeze blew his salt and pepper hair. "You, Chance, will be our bodyguard, if we need one." Billowing cumulous filled the Cuzco sky. Still no rain.

"I can be that," said Chance.

"I'm going to my room now," said Ed. "I have some calls to make." He staggered the slightest with his first step. Hoped they did not notice. "Call me as soon as Randy returns. Time is of the essence."

9 Desperate Parents

Randy showed his IBM credentials once again to the guard at the BCP headquarters. Filled out again the visiting journal. He did not lie to the question – Reason for visit? He simply scribbled the catchall "Consulting."

Pani met him at his office door with a question.

"Why have you returned? I thought you said . . ."

"I've thought it over, Pani," Randy said, shaking the man's soft hand. "I may be able to help you after all. Try, that is. But I need your assurance, first, that you will never tell anyone that I did so, especially not my manager."

"I will never tell a soul."

"And I need to emphasize that I promise myself nothing, only that I will try my best to find Daniel."

"I understand. And I am grateful." He pulled Randy close and hugged him. Tears of gratitude shown in his eyes. Randy was embarrassed by the feel of the bony man inside the expensive suit, and his heart broke a bit to think how Pani must feel. Maybe this was not a good idea after all. To get Pani's hopes up. Who was this Ed, anyway, with his so-called "connections." But he couldn't turn around and leave. Not now. Not after saying he would help. "Do you have time to answer some questions?"

"Come in, come in," said Pani, drawing his slick black bangs back with his hand. "Take a seat. I will answer all your questions to the best of my humble ability."

Pani's wife Ester came straight over. She was taller than Pani, in her heels, with a pale Spanish face, long braided hair, dangling silver earrings and a silver necklace. She had a twitch in her left eye, whenever Randy looked at her. He noticed too the tremor in her long fingers as she handed him a dozen copies of Daniel's school picture, and copies of his birth certificate with his little footprints at the top. And lastly she handed him Daniel's school outfit, one just like the one he was wearing the day he disappeared.

"Of course we have a private detective searching," she snapped, when Randy asked what actions they had taken besides contact the police. "And I have personally visited all the hospitals and orphanages in the Cuzco area."

"You say he was on a field trip with his school?"

"They were just up the road, at the ruins of Sacsahuaman. He was taking part in a community effort organized by the INC, the Culture Institute. They were cleaning the Inca stonework. He loved his Inca heritage."

"And no one noticed what happened?"

"No. His teacher said he was there one minute and gone the next. The organizers searched hours for him. Thought he might have fallen and hit his head. Or simply wandered off. Called us finally and the police and we searched all night. The police, family, friends. In all we searched the ruins two full days and nights."

"Two awful days and nights," said Pani. "An unending nightmare. Finally we agreed he was not in the ruins. That he had been taken. We waited for a ransom note, but no."

"He just disappeared," said Ester. Randy could see the woman was near her breaking point. What a mother must feel, to have lost a child and not know if he was alive or dead? If she would ever see him again.

"Only child?" he asked.

Pani nodded. "A special child," said Ester, lifting her chin. "He gave the best hugs in the world." She broke into tears. Randy bit his lips, imagined little Daniel beside his mother, giving him one of his special hugs.

"I'll be honest," said Randy. "I have no business looking for

48

your son. But I will because you have asked me. But I can't look for him forever. A week. Maybe two."

"We understand," said Pani.

"You are our last hope," said Ester. Her thin lips attempted a smile.

"I am going to try to help, just as your friends and the police tried to help. And I may fail, as your friends and the police have so far failed. But I am going to try. I promise you that."

"That's all we ask," said Pani. "Try as you did in India."

To hell with India, thought Randy, taking his leave. This is Peru and I don't have a clue.

10 Take my Picture?

The next day Kalene followed patiently behind Fernanda as she went from one brightly dressed, humorously be-hatted Inca woman to another.

"Take my picture?" they said invariably. "Pay what you wish."

Kalene remained quiet as Fernanda spoke to them in Spanish, a language she herself spoke, she spoke so many languages, living and dead. She nodded when the women protested that there were a million children in Cuzco, how could they remember this one? She pretended sadness when they expressed concern that he was missing.

At any time she could have passed the boy's scented shirt to the hairless hounds of Cuzco, those sacred dogs from the underworld. Asked them to track the boy. For she could talk to dogs, those faithful interested companions of man. She could talk to any animal. Because of where she came from. But she decided to be patient, to see where this all led. Hanuman had taught her that, if nothing else. That enjoyment could be had in watching them flounder about, on their own, without any assistance. She would let Fernanda go through the motions of helping. Asking the native women. The women from the high mountains who'd come down to beg, in their way. Let Fernanda continue her hopeless search.

Missing children? Yes the women had heard stories. They even knew a woman whose little girl was taken. Whose heart was broken. Kat was her name. Find Kat. She could tell them about her own child's abduction.

They could not find Kat. Look as they must.

The market, she sells today.

So they walked *Portal Belen*, passed under the old arch on the other side of *Plaza de Armas* to the *Mercado Central de Don Pedro*, a covered market with its rows and rows of wooden stalls selling fresh squeezed juice and chicken soup. So heathy, that smell. They questioned a few of the cooks whose eyes reflected the disappointment of a no sale. They moved deeper into the market, to the booths of llama-printed woven caps, sweaters and blankets, of cheap Inca chess sets and silver jewelry filled with semi-precious stones. Dark men, women and children manned the booths, eating rice and potato dishes from plastic plates. They looked up with hope, waved over Fernanda and Kalene, only to be shown the picture and hear the questions.

"No thank you," said Fernanda. "Have you seen this boy? We're looking for him. *Han visto este nino? Esta perdido. Lo han visto?*

No, they told her. They had not seen him. They knew nothing about him. No, no and no. Find Kat, one vender told her. Hours of searching, of asking, and nothing. Fernanda could not even find Kat.

They reached the section of fresh vegetables, a hundred different varieties of potatoes, tiny bananas and avocadoes big as melons. Next came the meat section, where rows of skinned chickens lay, sharp pronged feet projected out as if attacking. Kalene stopped, fascinated by a pan of cow hearts, stacked neatly, next to three severed goat heads with their tongues sticking out. Fernanda pulled at her gently to come on.

They stepped outside the market, where they asked shoppers coming in and those leaving the market.

"Have you seen this boy?" They had not. Kalene could tell that Fernanda was ready to give up. She was just about to suggest calling out the hairless hounds, when she felt a pair of eyes on her from below.

"You are not his mother," said a chubby woman seated by the market entrance. She wore a tall square hat over weary eyes. A small pile of black corn on the cob sat on a threadbare cloth before her.

"No," said Fernanda. "We are friends of the parents."

"He is high class. That is why he was chosen. They always

choose high class, healthy children."

"What?" said Fernanda, leaning down. "Who chose him? What do you know?"

"He is gone. You can't get him back." The woman looked away.

"Are you Kat?" asked Kalene.

The woman grunted something. Could have been "Yes."

"They took your child?" asked Fernanda.

The woman's face went blank.

"Two years ago," she said finally. "When I was high class. Before my life ended."

"I'm sorry," said Fernanda.

"We're sorry," said Kalene, fascinated that Fernanda had actually succeeded in finding the famous Kat.

"Can you tell us? What you know?"

"Buy my corn," she told them, indicating the few cobs on the ground before her.

Fernanda gave her 20 US dollars, ten times the value of the corn, and squatted down to hear what she could tell them.

"The Gods want us to sacrifice, to kill the things we love," she told them, crumpling the bill in her fist before putting it away in her apron.

Kalene noticed Fernanda's body shake at the declaration.

"You know?" said Kat. "I can tell by your reaction. You know what I am talking about."

"No, no I don't know," said Fernanda. "Please tell me what you mean."

"*She* knows," said Kat, indicating Kalene. "I see it in her eyes."

"Maybe," said Kalene. "But tell us anyway."

Kat leaned back against the wall. Kalene noticed the pitchfork veins on the back of her hands. Wondered if she was not Kat at all, but some kind of demoness trying to mislead them. Were there others at play in the larger game, the one that had brought Kalene to Arkansas, to find Fernanda? She liked the direction this was taking. If a boy was to be sacrificed, why not a woman alongside him? A woman too full of love to remain on this earth.

"The old ways didn't die," Kat said. "As much as the Spanish tried with their crosses and saints and 50,000 churches. With their torture and slavery and murder. What they did not know, what I know now, is that even if the masses stop praying, stop believing, their Gods don't die. They still demand their due."

"What do you mean?" asked Fernanda. "Please, a boy's life is at stake."

"A sacrifice," Kat said. "He will be sacrificed as my daughter was sacrificed. At the solstice. As always. To ensure the rains come, that the harvest will be good. There is nothing you can do. There is nothing you should do."

Kalene and Fernanda looked at each other.

"But who will sacrifice him? Who was it that killed your little girl?" said Fernanda.

"The ones who keep the Gods happy," she said. "The Wari."

Ah, thought Kalene. Just the people I am looking for.

"When is this solstice you mentioned?" asked Fernanda.

"What is today?" the woman asked back. Fernanda told her. "Three days," the woman said then. "In three days the boy will be dead."

11 Connections

Ed took an Advil, dry, while his boss rattled on. "What the hell are you up to down there? I send you on a simple tail and next thing I know you want to use our staff to research Cuzco child abductions. Has birdwatching driven you cuckoo?"

"I know it doesn't make sense on your end," said Ed, his voice breaking a bit. "But I think there may be a connection." He looked around the spotless room, sniffed the scent of Clorox.

"To mutilations and murders in India? I'm not seeing this, Ed."

"Trust me, boss. Trust me. Can you get me the data? Any open cases, leads, etc?" Outside his window he could hear the chatter and laughter of children. Their school shoes clattered on the stone steps as they skipped down.

"I'll run it through Intel. If you are sure it is related to the

Indian Ripper case."

"I think it may be. That's why I need the data." Ed paused, feeling the Advil make its candy coated way down his esophagus. "What do you think I am doing here in Peru? Freelancing?"

His boss laughed at the suggestion. "No. I guess not. So is the bird acting normal? No inclination to eat human flesh?"

"Not so far," said Ed. His head pounded. He wished he could be a bird himself and fly away from the pain. But he had a boy to find first. "I have to go."

"So the birdwatching cover has worked for you?"

"Like a charm. Cause I love birdwatching so much."

"Sure you do. Birds with two long legs. I'll have the info emailed tonight."

"Thanks, boss. I appreciate your trust. You were always a good man to work for." And he hung up.

12 Chance's precious find in Pisac

While Randy did computer research on the newly formed World Wide Web, checking out chatrooms and bulletin boards for mention of stolen children in Peru, while the girls showed pictures and questioned Inca women in the streets, while birdwatcher ex-private eye Ed did who knows what with his so-called connections, Chance took a taxi to Pisac, a smaller scenic town below ruins in the mountains about an hour away.

The street led uphill through the city, looping round past auto part stores and bakeries and wedding dress shops jammed together. A scattering of pedestrians, workers, mothers and kids. Dogs sniffed in piles of rubbish.

They passed over one hill then another, the city stretching below now, visible through the treetops. Ahead of them higher mountains. Below them a stream appeared.

He'd heard he could find good samples of Peruvian pyrite in Pisac. Cube-shaped, naturally sparkling golden crystals. Fool's gold.

Rockhounds and novices loved fool's gold. Would pay good money. And here in Peru he was sure he could get the stones cheap.

The taxi dropped him at a metal bridge next to the town center. He passed the main street and saw the sign for the market. He headed up a long narrow lane which opened into the main square with the market stalls covered by blue canopies. Green terraces, built five hundred years ago, towered over the square. Chance spotted rocks sparkling on one of the tables and headed over.

"How much?" he asked a curvy young lady dressed in a gray wool sweater with coral buttons. Ah nothing like a tight sweater to accentuate a woman's boppers. She stood behind a wood table strewn with natural pyrite crystals, polished pyrite balls, quartz crystals and mineral combinations he had only seen online. Museum quality pieces.

"They twinkle like your eyes," he told her, indicating the pyrite.

"Fool's gold," she said, smiling back. He asked her to decide which were her best pieces. She selected a dozen of the pyrite balls. He bought them all, after arguing her down a bit, marvelously polished balls with crystals sparkling from tiny caves. Heavy balls. He could feel magic in that weight, as he gripped them.

"They're almost as heavy as mine," he said.

"What?" she said.

"My balls. These are almost as heavy as mine."

The vender gave him a strange look like she didn't understand, but he knew she did.

Chance would turn these stones into money. Twice what he paid. Sold retail, in the States.

"Where they come from?" he asked her, as she wrapped up the stones. "The pyrite."

She pointed towards the hills and said something that he did not grasp at first. "My mean," it sounded like. He would need time with her, to extract what she knew about the pyrite's location.

"You are an Inca treasure," he told her. "Will you have lunch with me?" He made the motion of scooping food into his mouth, pointed at her and him.

She smiled. "Such foolishness." But she called over a friend to watch her table and went with the large American.

She took him past the square, down the narrow stone street with magnificent Inca terraces above their heads. Like they were walking below a giant's walled garden. Took him into a small new restaurant with clay pots of tall stemmed flowers that attracted enormous black bumblebees. Chance dodged one that buzzed his nose, as he took a seat across from this fellow seller of treasure from the veins of the earth.

The only other patrons were a couple in the corner next to a pile of overstuffed trek-size backpacks. The boy, in his twenties, had tie-die hair and appeared to be dressed in his pajamas. The girl wore a tangerine, formless dress. On her head a souvenir wool cap with flaps over her ears made her look Russian. They both looked bored. As if they did not know what to do next.

"My name is Maria," the vender told him. She had a nice smile.

"I'm Chance."

"Good luck or the bad kind?" she said.

"For you to find out."

She ordered purple chicha and avocado salad for the two of them, then turned her attention to Chance.

"What do you do?" she asked him.

"For a living? I own a quartz crystal mine back in the states, a mine with the clearest crystal in the world," he told her. "Quartz crystal that could hold a wavelength forever. Crystal once used in radios and radar, in the 30s and 40s, crystal that helped to win the last world war."

The subject fascinated her, he could tell by the way she leaned towards him, he could tell by the widening of her smile. He described his mine to her, then, over the whir of the blender in the kitchen.

And deftly switched the subject to her own mine. The one here in the Andes. Her pyrite mine. Her mine of fool's gold. But she kept putting him off.

"Not big mine," she told him. "Very small. Only me work it."

He took one of her pieces from his bag.

"These stones are perfect," he told her. "I've never seen such fine material, such artistry. And I've been in the crystal business for years."

"Yes," she told him. "As if they fell from heaven."

After their avocado salads, and ten chichas, six for him and four for her, after she told him a bit about herself, about her desire to go to the states one day, he managed to get her started drawing a map to her mine on the cloth napkin. The restaurant owner protested – he gave her a twenty and shooshed her away.

Chance traced the lines on the map, entranced by the sureness in which she drew each one. He wondered how rugged the terrain was, where she had marked the X. Could he get a truck up there? His hand brushed against hers, a fine small hand with its own map of thin veins. She laughed, moved her hand, he followed where she moved. Finished with the drawing, she held up the napkin. He applauded. It was a good map, with the roads (or were they simply paths?) all named, all laid down by her confident hand. She had even circled one place, writing in the words, "Shining Path." Ah, he really wanted to see that path. Probably a quartz vein full of virgin crystals.

"No go," she said. "Not there."

"Oh you don't have to," he told her. "I will go alone, Maria."

Conversation slowed. He thought of the photo in the front of his pack, pulled it out and lay it before her on the table.

"Have you seen this boy?"

Her smile froze. "No," she said. "Why?"

"Oh, no reason," he told her. "He's gone missing, that's all."

He paid for the meal and walked her back towards the plaza, his arm around her. When they passed the hotel on the corner, he slowed.

"You want to rest with me?" he asked her, indicating the hotel. He could tell she was hesitating, taking time to consider what he was asking her, really, he saw it in her eyes. He hesitated himself, wanting to quickly close the deal. He pulled out a twenty. She stepped back. He offered her forty.

Mistake. He could see it in her dark eyes.

But wait, she stepped closer and took the money. Chance started to smile but she put her hand, the one with the money, on his mouth, stopping him. Her hand passed over his lips, up to the jagged line that scarred his otherwise handsome face. Tears appeared in her eyes, eyes that locked on his.

"You are not good luck or bad luck," said Maria. He smelled the sweet chicha on her breath, saw how her eyes searched for something in his that was not there. "You are sad luck," she told him. Her hand dropped from his face. The two twenties he'd given her slipped to the gutter. He watched, speechless, as this precious Peruvian girl turned from him and walked slowly back to her ordinary life, selling semi-precious stones to the hapless tourists, there at her table, at the market, forever in the shadow of the ruins.

He had insulted her. Lost his chance. Why was he so dumb, at times? Too much beer, he supposed. Too impatient.

He walked back to the river road, turned left to the taxi stand. Showed the first driver his treasure map, the map to the pyrite mine that Maria had drawn for him. The taxi driver rolled up his window and locked his doors. Chance went to the next driver in the line. The man took one look at the map and started yelling at the other drivers. Something in Spanish. Or was it that other language they spoke?

Chance put the map away, gave up asking them to take him to the mine. He asked instead for a ride back to Cuzco. One of the drivers, a well-dressed young man in an unmarked car, said that he would take him to the city for thirty soles, about ten dollars. Chance climbed in, setting his heavy pack in the other passenger seat, the pack full of fool's gold from a girl he could not buy, from a mine he might never find, lost in the Andes mountains. Somewhere up there near a shining path. He had the map in his pocket, what good that did him.

The driver put in a cassette tape. Chance liked the first song, a woman lamenting in Spanish about a man who broke her heart.

Several songs later the taxi passed a sign indicating the ruins of Sacsahuaman. Chance remembered that that was where the boy was lost. He turned to see the mighty grey structures, built with 30 ton stones neatly fitted in place. All roofless. Abandoned. The road took a twist, a dogleg, he lost view of the ruins. The taxi bounced over a pile of dirt in the road, bounced again over a hole as they drove down, down, to the sprawling city of Cuzco. Where the others must be searching for the boy. In vain, he feared.

13 Randy eyes the World

Randy wondered how Fernanda and Kalene were doing as he sat at his laptop computer, connected by modem to the IBM network and thereby the worldwide web, performing his virtual search for information on lost and abducted children in Peru. He hit chatrooms and postboards all over the world. Such a search would have been impossible a few years ago, a blessing of the new worldwide network of computers. But you had to know what sites to visit, what boards to peruse. Not just anyone could search the worldwide web with success. Pani had been right about that.

Incredible to traverse the world, communicating with people on subjects of interest, without even getting out of your seat. If only he could communicate so easily, in person, with Fernanda. Something was bothering her, since India. Not the affair he'd had with Julie. That was a secret he still held from her. Would never confide to her. But something else. Almost as if a dark shadow had followed her from India. A shadow on her soul.

And not just a shadow, the FBI had called her in, grilled her on where she went and what she did and who she met in India. Surely they didn't suspect that she had anything to do with the mutilation of her teacher, at the ashram in Rishikesh? Fernanda? Little horse-riding Fernanda who wouldn't hurt a fly? She hadn't even wanted to go to India. He had practically forced her. He thought she would like Varanasi. So very strange how your best intentions can turn on you.

At least she had a friend with her on this trip, young Kalene. What a strange person, so much energy, her eyes darting about, like a bird on high, looking for prey. Was there more to her than she appeared? He wondered how long before Chance bedded her. Brought her down to earth.

And this Ed fellow. Randy wondered why he had been so easily swayed by Ed's "I have connections, I can help you find the boy" argument. Ed did come across as someone you could trust. A man of convictions. Randy was risking his career, though, hiding from IBM his true task here in Peru, and no one seemed to care. What did they have to lose by going on this goose chase? Some time? He had his career to lose, a successful career he had spent years achieving. He was proud to work for a world leader in IT like IBM. He was proud to be a programmer. He never intended to be a detective, a crime solver. This was not his forte.

He puzzled over his predicament, as he chased a thread,

repeated on other network sites, about natives in the high Andes who still practiced sacrifices to their gods. Mostly they sacrificed llamas. White ones when they could get them. Their witch doctors, their shamans, would take out the heart and guts and read the road to the future in the map of the veins. Apparently, long ago, they occasionally sacrificed children as well. But that ended with the arrival of Christianity.

A dead end. If only someone would improve searching content on postboards. Maybe IBM would write a program that searched them all of them at once, from a single place. That's an idea!

He killed his connection, and closed down his computer.

Thirsty, he went to the bar and took a seat.

"A sour," he told the barman.

Two bearded men sat down on the balcony and began to argue. Something about the ruins. They acted like scientists, or university professors, so serious and headstrong. They spoke English, but each with a different accent. Randy's ears perked up when he heard the words "mountain tribes."

He decided to query them on the subject. He got down off his stool, drink in hand, and walked over.

"Excuse me," he said, standing in front of their table. "I couldn't help overhearing your conversation. The subject of mountain tribes is of great interest to me. I have a question."

The men looked at each other, both curious.

"Yes?" said the one in glasses.

"Well, two questions. First, are you scientists?"

"Archeologists, actually. Participating in a dig."

"Cool," said Randy, pulling up a chair. "I am an IBM programmer, here on assignment."

"Fine. Fine," said the one with no glasses. "So what is your second question?"

"Are there mountain tribes in Peru, any that you know of, that still practice human sacrifice?"

"No," he said without a pause.

"Oh yes there are," said Mr glasses. "I've heard of recent cases. In fact, a case made the Lima paper a couple of years ago."

"Absurd," said Mr no glasses. "Admit you're pulling our legs."

Rain began to fall, forcing them to shuffle their chairs out of reach of the drops.

"I'm serious," said Mr glasses. "People think the Incas began human sacrifices on their own when they came to power, but it was the Wari tribe that taught the Incas the art. A thousand years ago. Mostly *child* sacrifice. At the winter and summer solstices. As in the old days, these people still search out the most beautiful, healthy children in the land, steal them and hold them, fattening them for weeks like your American farmers fatten a turkey before Thanksgiving. Then they march the children to the mountain tops, strangle them unconscious or drug them and bury them in the snow with offerings of chicha and tiny statues of llamas. For the Sun God Inti, for the Moon God Mama Killa, for the God of nature Pachamama. For all the mountain spirits. In this way they bribe the coming of the rains for their crops, the prevention of earthquakes that shatter their homes. In this way they pray to the Gods to keep the world spinning, the sky blue, the grass green. Perhaps we owe them for this rain falling now."

"I will not believe such nonsense," said Mr no glasses.

"Stop the sacrifices, and catastrophes will come," said Mr glasses. "The world as we know it would end. This is what they still believe, isolated as they are in their high mountain homes."

Randy nodded. Thanked the men. He had uncovered a rich vein of knowledge here, with much implication. Was it possible that little Daniel had been abducted for such a sacrifice? Were his abductors fattening him up at this very moment? Randy searched online to see when the next solstice would occur. Three days. Was it possible? Did they have three days, and three days only to find the child before he was taken to the top of a mountain and fed to the Inca gods?

14 Puzzle pieces coming together

An exuberant, dripping wet Fernanda slipped, as she ran up the hotel steps, aiming for Randy's arms. He just caught her before her head hit the ground.

"Whoa there!" he said, feeling the chilly drops strike his shirt and soak through. He pulled her up with him on the step. Next to them, the middle-aged round-faced candy vender covered the goodies on her cart with clear plastic.

"Randy," Fernanda said close to his ear. "The boy is alive. And I know who has him!"

"The Wari have him," said Kalene, running up behind Fernanda, looking mousey with her hair flattened around her skull by the rain. "They intend to kill him!"

"The Wari?" said Randy, and he had to laugh. "I was just going to tell you the same thing." He opened the door. "Let's go inside and find Ed. See what he has to say."

From the restaurant balcony, an hour later, Randy saw Chance get out of a taxi and heft his pack onto his back. He called for him to come and join them.

Chance walked up to the crowded table, obviously curious as to who everyone was.

"Ah, Mr Chance, just in time," said Ed. "Seems we may need your muscle sooner rather than later."

Chance straddled a chair next to Kalene, and set down his heavy pack. Kalene grabbed it like a child would, and looked inside.

"Wow," she said, seeing the sparkle of gold.

"Later," whispered Chance.

"These are Daniel's parents, Pani and Ester."

Chance stood back up and shook their hands. The woman, elegant as she was, looked exhausted. A failing spirit.

"And this is Isabel from INC, the National Institute of Culture. She is a friend of the family and Daniel's godmother."

Pleasant looking, around forty, she had the long angular face and v-shape nostrils of some of the indigenous people Randy had seen in Cuzco. A noble look about her. "I'm here to help in any way I can."

"Pleased to meet you," Chance said to her. Randy could hear Chance's nervous energy in his voice. He felt the same way.

"We have reached a conclusion," said Ed, measuring the woman. "A conclusion based on facts we uncovered today. Facts that lead us to believe that little Daniel may have been abducted by an ancient race of people. A people who live in the mountains, who follow the old ways."

"My people," said Isabel from INC. "The proud Wari."

"You've found the boy?" asked Chance, his mouth wide open.

"No," said Randy. "But clues that point us in a certain direction."

Randy studied Chance. What was his pal thinking? Were they serious? Was this just wishful thinking?

"We believe the boy was taken to be sacrificed," said Fernanda.

Chance sat down with a thud. "What do you mean?"

Isabel, the woman from INC, spoke now. "My people have always believed in tithing to the Gods. Just like Christians tithe to their God. Only we tithe by sacrificing our best. The Incas, when they took over, adopted our tradition, after we explained to them how necessary it was. In the old days, our sacrifices included the sacrifice of our most beautiful, most heathy children. For the good of all. Your friends here believe that my people still practice this abomination." She indicated the gang.

"My contacts confirm," said Ed, swallowing hard, then continuing, "that every year, early June and early December, a few weeks before each solstice, going back as far as certain records go, one or two well-off children have been reported missing here in Cuzco. No ransom note. No call. Never heard from again. They just disappear."

"My online research didn't indicate that," said Randy, "but then I met some archaeologists here in the hotel. One of them told me the Wari were likely culprits. That they still practice human sacrifice during the winter and summer solstice."

"Which I say is not true," said Isabel, lifting her chin.

"We actually talked to a woman whose daughter disappeared," said Fernanda. "She's the one told us who did it. The Waris, she said, the Wari people sacrificed my little girl."

"She's crazy to be saying such things," said Isabel. "I know my people."

"Why don't we go to the police and tell them all this?" asked Chance.

"No," said Pani. "They won't believe you. They say it was Shining Path guerrillas. That he is lost for good."

Ester pulled out a handkerchief and brought it to her cheek.

"The problem is," said Ed, "that this is our best lead. It is up to us to chase it down. And we only have three days before the next solstice. We need to visit these people in the mountains. We need to go where these people live. Make sure that they do not have the boy."

"Ha," said Isabel. "As if you could drive right up there. It is a two day hard hike to the main settlement. On the old Inca Trail. At 3,900 meters. Nearly 13,000 feet."

"We'll need to be outfitted," said Daniel's father Pani. "Maybe horses, mules? A guide. Porters."

"Yes, *we* would need to be outfitted," said Ed, indicating the gang. "But you need to stay here in Cuzco, Pani. With Ester. In case someone calls about your son. In case you are needed by the police. In case you are needed by Ester."

Pani looked at Ester, who simply looked to the ground.

"How much would such outfitting cost?" asked Ed to Isabel.

"Look," said Isabel. "I have an idea. Just so happens I was planning to leave tomorrow for the settlement. To take part in our solstice celebration. Which has nothing to do with human sacrifice, by the way. I already have outfitters. You could join me for, let's say, a thousand dollars. To cover extra porters, food and equipment. I'll take you to the village, be your interpreter, and prove to you, once and for all, that they don't have Daniel."

"Can you cover our expenses?" Ed asked to Pani.

"Yes. Of course I will pay," said Pani.

"Ok then. We leave quite early in the morning," said Isabel. "We may spend two nights camping on the trail, depending on your endurance. The hike to the village is part Inca Trail, part Wari. High, hard mountain hiking. Thousands upon thousands of ancient steps. One or all or you will likely get altitude sickness."

"But there's something to take for that, no?" said Ed. "Coca leaves?"

"Yes," said Isabel. "Coca can help. Coca gum, candy, leaves."

"When is this solstice thing again?" asked Chance.

"In three days," said Randy. "If Daniel has been taken by the Wari, and we don't know that for sure, but if he has been taken by them, we only have three days to save him."

Ester got up, covering her face. "Excuse me. Please." She left the balcony.

"Arrange everything for them, Isabel, please" said Pani, who then raced after his wife.

"Damn," said Chance. "You really think they have the boy?"

"I almost hope so," said Ed. "For if they don't, then I fear he is lost, forever."

Everyone let that sink in. Chance knocked his knuckles nervously on the table.

"I think you are wrong about all this," said Isabel. "But I will arrange a bus to pick you up at four in the morning. For the drive to the Inca trailhead." She turned to the women. "Are you planning to go too?"

"Yes!" said Fernanda and Kalene in unison.

"Then you need to buy hiking boots. You men too. And rain jackets. And hats. I'll make a list." She scribbled on a piece of paper from her purse and handed the note to Ed. "Now if you'll excuse me. I have calls to make and packing to do."

"So we can come with you?" asked Fernanda, obviously pleased with the idea.

"Of course," Isabel said, her long sharp nose pointing from one to the other of them. "Though it may be the hardest walk you ever take, I'd love to have you along."

ELSE

Part Two: The Journey

ELSE

15 An Early Start

"Ok this is way too early to get up," moaned Chance in the back of the minibus. In the dark.

Ed agreed. After a frantic shopping trip the evening before, to get the right clothes for trekking, he had slept little. Tossing and turning, arguing with his wife's voice, the one in his head, the one that insisted he was too sick and old to go off mountain climbing. He had no good argument against that voice, against his dead wife, except to tell her that he wanted to go. That this might be his last good walk on the earth. And there was the boy. He couldn't ignore the need to search for the boy. Even if it led him to the top of a mountain. After all, he was FBI. He was the only trained officer in the group. He had to go, despite his illness. And what about "the bird?" What about Fernanda? He had orders to tail her and she was going on the trek. He had to follow his orders, no matter where they led.

Five hours, maybe, he had slept, before "Up, get up!" A

female voice at his hotel door, an insistent knocking. The INC woman he supposed. Isabel. He did not trust that woman. All women by the age of forty knew too much, were too conniving. They had learned how to get their way by then, over men. How to nag them, how to humiliate them. Men only knew how to think straight while a woman, especially an older woman, knew how to think in ten directions at once. They knew how to say things evil and loving in the same breath. The fact that such a woman was ripping him from a sleep he had finally managed to reach made him like her all the less. "Get up!" he heard her call to someone else down the hall. "The bus leaves in 10 minutes. With or without you."

Ah, so she is already trying to take over, he thought, and used that thought to motivate himself to get out of bed. This was his expedition, not hers, or so he told himself. He dressed, grabbed the gear and hustled downstairs to the bus in the dead silence of a Cuzco night. He sat in front, and wondered what the hell he was doing. I'm too old, he thought, I'm dying. I know nothing about trekking. What kind of a leader could I possibly make?

"Too damn early," complained Chance, and Ed agreed.

The bus jerked forward, all seats full with the gang and strange little Peruvian men. The seven dwarves? But then who was Snow White? Fernanda? Within minutes most fell asleep in their seats, leaning back with mouths open, or forward with bobbing heads. Ed did not sleep. He sat envisioning scenes from his past, vivid scenes that pierced the dark more brilliantly than the feeble headlights of the bus. His wife's sickness. The days she seemed her normal thinking self, then other days when she couldn't remember how to put on her shoes. When he had to dress her. He tried to be patient, but sometimes he lost it. Snapped like you would at a four year old, and feel terrible after. The look in her eyes, when he finally gave up and took her to that rest home. Her eyes pleading, accusing. Him helpless to save her.

The bus jerked to a halt. The driver cursed at a hairless dog taking its time to cross the road. Ed watched as the chubby driver wrestled the tall stickshift back into first. The bus lurched forward, once, twice, rocking those awakened back to sleep. Ed continued his musings.

How many times had he struggled in life, only to fail? So many unsolved cases. What did he have to show, in the end? Would it be enough, finding the boy, to say he had made a difference? That he had succeeded at life after all? He doubted it.

16 The Inca Trailhead

After a few hours' drive, the last thirty minutes spent bouncing in the ruts of a narrow cliff-side cart-path overlooking the wild rapids of the Wilkanuta River, harrowing miles tying knots in Randy's stomach, finally they reached the end of the road. Literally. Only mountainous footpaths from here on.

They climbed out of the bus and stretched. Zipped up their jackets. The mountain air at the trailhead, next to the boulder-filled river, had a bite as cold as snow. Randy hoped the sun would finish rising soon.

The porters, dark, a bit rough looking, except for the cook Paro with his intelligent eyes, unloaded the tents and cooking equipment from the top of the minibus. They spoke to each other in a strange language as they did so. Randy asked Isabel about them, as he watched the porters try their best to keep to themselves. To be invisible.

"Quechua," Isabel explained. "They speak mostly Quechua.

The original language of my people. Of all native people in this region. For a thousand years."

Isabel supervised the porters as they made towering packs that they balanced on their backs. She handed out copies of a map she'd made of the trails they'd take to the Wari settlement, marked with the place she hoped they would camp the first night of the trek. She told Randy and the gang to only carry the minimum in their backpacks, water, snacks and raingear, to give any large or heavy items to the porters.

"Your legs will thank me in an hour," she told them, as she directed them out of the village, across a wood and iron bridge standing high over the rapids which dashed around boulders the size of houses.

"The end of the new world," said Isabel, taking the lead at the head of the trail. "From here it will be a foot path of dirt and then stone trails, Inca and Wari-built. They wind for miles up into the mountains, into the cloud forest. We'll do one mountain pass today, past ruins of villages and forts built during our golden age. We'll stay on the main trail for Machu Picchu most of today, then turn off towards the Wari settlement."

"So it is a two days' march?" asked Ed. He placed a hand to his head and frowned, as if he had a headache.

"Well," she said. "Two and a half maybe for this group."

"Why didn't we bring horses?" said Ed.

"The trail is no good, in places, for horses," she said. "Remember my people did not have horses back then. So we walk."

The sun broke through the clouds. Randy felt the warmth of it through his jacket. Around them, clusters of grain at the top of the high weeds caught the light and shone like little lanterns. He pointed out the phenomenon to Fernanda.

"We are walking in a fairytale," said Fernanda.

"Only a matter of time before the wood nymphs come out," said Chance.

"And chew off our toes," said Kalene.

They had plenty of energy for useless chatter. Later they would measure the energy they wasted on talk.

"You can take the Inca and Wari trails all the way to Ecuador, or south to Bolivia," said Isabel. "Or over the mountains to the Amazon jungle."

"The Amazon jungle?" said Randy. "I thought the Amazon was in Brazil."

"Here in the south, and in the north too, we have jungle. The Amazon basin jungle, to be more precise. Land of the Ashaninkas."

"Real jungle?" asked Fernanda. Already Randy could see she

was breathing deeply. The altitude.

"Real jungle," said Isabel. "Panthers, monkeys, macaws and parrots."

"And hummingbirds," Randy said, looking to Ed to see if that got a rise from him.

Ed did not react. He stayed steadfastly on the heels of Isabel. Randy and Fernanda came next. Chance and Kalene brought up the rear, not counting the seven dwarves with their tall packs.

As the trail began to ascend, they passed their first ruins. Down below them, beside the river. Not much more than a few interconnected, abandoned stone houses.

"Amazon army ants," said Randy. "I remember stories. An old movie with Stewart Granger. How they travel in millions, devouring every living plant and animal in their path. Maybe that is what wiped out those Incas."

"No army ants in the mountains," said Ed.

"Thank goodness!" said Fernanda.

"Only maybe a few guerillas," said Isabel. "They're getting more bloodthirsty, as their numbers dwindle."

"Gorillas?" asked Chance. "Big hairy monkeys?"

"No of course not," said Isabel. "Rebels, you know. Men

fighting against the government."

"Oh," said Chance, but he looked puzzled. "Rebels killed off the Incas?"

Randy laughed. "Go back to sleep Chance."

Clumps of cactus appeared along the dusty trail.

Isabel stopped by one of the plants, pointed out strange white sores in its green skin. "Look, you guys," she said. They gathered round as she reached into one of the sores and pulled out a small beetle. She smashed the beetle with her finger nails, releasing a crimson liquid.

"Blood?" asked Ed.

"Carmine acid," she said. "From the cochineal bug. Used in the modern world for food coloring and lipstick. Textile dye as well. Come here," she said to Kalene.

Kalene stepped closer. Isabel painted a war paint stripe on her cheek with the brilliant colored liquid. She smashed another bug, and created two more slashes of red on Kalene's face. Fernanda got the makeup mirror from the pack to show her. Kalene admired herself.

"Those stripes make you look demonic," said Chance.

"Ah, then it brings out the best in me," said Kalene, slugging Chance in the shoulder. He winced at her punch.

"You throw a mean curve," he said.

"If you only knew."

Argh, thought Randy. Chance is asking for it, and so is Kalene. Not good. Not good at all. Poor Crystal back in Arkansas. But she knew what she was getting into when she stole Chance from Fernanda.

Isabel had them move to the side of the trail so the porters could pass. Randy noticed Paro and a couple of others stuffing green leaves into their mouths from plastic bags and chewing as they marched along. He watched as they disappeared up the twisting trail, spitting out stems.

"What were those leaves they were eating?" Randy asked Isabel as the group set out again in single and double file. "Some kind of tea leaves?"

"Coca leaves," Ed answered in her place. "They like to chew coca leaves. It gives them energy. But, yes, they make tea from the leaves as well. And candy. Here in Peru."

"Oh that's right, you mentioned that yesterday."

"We shall have some coca tea at lunch," said Isabel. "Good for altitude sickness."

"Coca?" said Randy. "Like Coca-Cola?"

"More like cocaine," said Ed. "In small doses. Cocaine is

made from coca leaves. You are right too about Coca-Cola, though. Coca-Cola was made from the same leaves, originally. Made with the active ingredient of cocaine. And from Kola nuts they extracted caffeine to add as well. Around 1900 though the American government forbid the Coke Company from getting all of America addicted to their drink."

Randy and the others laughed.

"The government made the makers of Coca-Cola take out the addictive cocaine component while allowing them to still use denatured coca leaves for flavoring. As far as the addictiveness of caffeine, the government tried to have the makers of Coca-Cola remove that ingredient as well, but they failed. The rest is history."

"I don't like Coke, or any soda for that matter" said Randy, thinking, what a frigging encyclopedia. They should put this guy on the World Wide Web, and have him answer questions all day from around the world.

"You are in the minority," said Ed. "Most of the world is addicted. To Coke and other caffeine and sugar drinks. And those poor porters are addicted to coca leaves."

"And chicha," said Isabel. "The Inca and Wari people love their chicha."

17 Mapacho and Ayahuasca

Three hours into the trek and they had all shed their jackets.

A natural selection of who goes first became evident as Fernanda and Randy's pace slowed, both of them breathing hard. The open hillsides, hung with Spanish moss and large clinging flowers, changed to trees and vines and a stream babbling through the undergrowth. The trail narrowed. A vigorous Chance, in great shape after years of working in the quartz mine, made his way past Randy and Fernanda. He knew he could walk twice as fast, twice as far, as all of them combined.

Ed paused to take two Advil. Chance passed him as well and found himself next to the leader of the pack, next to Isabel. Kalene followed in his footsteps. He could have passed Isabel as well, but he didn't want to show off.

The path became smooth steps of one or more flat stones across, steps that tested the fitness of all of them at this altitude.

Across the wide valley, when they came over a rise, they could see mysterious plumes of thin clouds embracing the shoulders of mountains.

"Look," said Chance, stopping short. Kalene bumped into him. "Over there. Condors." The large birds spiraled on an updraft.

Isabel laughed. "No. Those are common vultures. Something is about to die."

"Ah," said Chance, starting up again. He liked a good walk but wasn't sure this was the best place to go walking. Especially with Kalene practically on his heels.

"We are in the cloud forest," said Isabel. "Often, early mornings, the clouds come between the trees, searching, searching. People get lost in that fog and are never found. Taken by Apu. The mountain spirit."

"And people live up here?" said Chance. "So far from town?"

"Here and much higher, above the cloud forest."

"What if they get sick?" said Kalene.

"There is the local shaman," said Isabel. "He will burn the plant Mapacho in his pipe and blow the spirit of the Mapacho, the smoke, over the sick person."

"And that helps?" said Kalene.

"Usually," said Isabel.

"And if that Mapacho smoke doesn't work?" asked Chance.

"Oh the shaman knows many cures. But if the sick one wants, they can hike or request to be carried two days to the doctor in town," said Isabel. She paused on the trail, apparently to give Randy and Fernanda and Ed a chance to catch up. "Most don't bother as they know if the shaman can't help them they will likely be dead by the time they reach town."

"Tell me something," said Chance.

"Yes?"

"We're wasting our time, aren't we?" he said. "Your people don't have the boy, do they?"

"No," she said. "They don't. But at least you can enjoy with us our solstice festivities when we reach the settlement," said Isabel. "Llama to eat and all the chicha you can drink."

"Sounds good to me," said Chance.

"And me," said Kalene.

Just then a woman appeared on the trail above them. A heavyset gal, she took up most of the trail. She had something, a baby perhaps, strapped on her back inside a colorful wool scarf. On her head she wore a black top hat, the kind popular for men in the 1800s.

Isabel said a few words to her, in that language of the local natives. The woman responded with a sigh and continued on her way down. Who knows how far she had come already. But one thing Chance knew, she had at least two hours to go before she reached town.

"And if one of us gets sick?" asked Chance, seeing Ed come into view, sweat pouring down his forehead. His eyes were ringed with fatigue, he hesitated before taking each step. Just looking at him made Chance feel half exhausted.

"Water," she told them as they gathered round her. "Please take out your water now and take a big drink. You are losing a lot of moisture breathing with open mouths."

They sat on the steps and did as she told them.

"The porters should already be setting up lunch for us. An hour uptrail."

Chance liked the sound of that. He had built quite an appetite getting up so early and then marching, at this altitude, for hours.

"Today's cook, my dear friend Paro, is a shaman actually. If any of you fall ill, he can treat you," she told them. "He is an excellent medicine man, as well as a good cook. He carries with him both Mapacho and Ayahuasca."

"Aya whats ka?" said Chance.

"Ayahuasca," said Isabel. "A plant that grows in the low mountains. A powerful hallucinogenic that allows Paro to do divinations. Some shamans use mescaline extract from the San Pedro Cactus, but Paro prefers Ayahuasca."

"He can see into the future?" asked Kalene.

"When he is under the spell of Ayahuasca, he says he can see the future as clearly as we see the trail before us. And if he looks at a person, he can see the taut string that ties them to their destiny."

Chance saw Kalene perk up at that. He wondered if she was new age. The kind that buy the healer crystals he sells in Arkansas. He had only talked with her a couple of times. A fun girl, if a little crazy. She would be good in the sack, he was sure of that. He wondered if he could lay her, on this trip, without his wife Crystal finding out. Fernanda had such a big mouth. Fernanda, Fernanda, Fernanda. Fernanda of the Mexican spirits and Indian mystics and troubled dreams. He did not understand Fernanda, and supposed he never would.

"Couldn't Paro go into a trance and just tell us where the boy is?" said Randy, appearing to have finally caught his breath. "Tell us what happened to Daniel?"

"If you wish I can ask him to ingest Ayahuasca tonight," said Isabel. "After dinner. It takes a lot out of him, but I understand why you would ask this of him."

"Yes, please," said Fernanda, sitting next to Randy, leaning her head on his shoulder. "In my homeland there are men who do such things."

"Okay, then," said Isabel. "Shall we continue?" Not waiting for a vote, which she may have lost, she rose.

18 Ed shows his gun

Fernanda felt very very tired. She never in her life climbed so many steps. At least the day was cool. That helped. Randy would stop, whenever she did, and have a seat with her on the boulders next to the trail, but she could tell he was growing impatient.

And Chance, she could kill Chance. He started singing, "*La cucaracha, la cucaracha, ya no quiere caminar.* Poor Fernanda, poor Fernanda, I don't think she's going far."

"Shut up, Chance," Randy said, but Chance continued to hum the song as he left them behind.

Am I risking a miscarriage? she wondered. With all this exertion. Walking so much. No, surely a mother's walking can't hurt the baby. He must be so small. Swimming around in my tummy. Randy Junior is probably enjoying the ride.

But if I start to hurt, I must tell him. Ask Randy to go down the mountain with me, allowing the others to go on. I'll have to. For the sake of the boy, little Daniel. She wondered how Daniel must feel, torn away from his family. Alone with strangers. They had to find him. Had to help him.

Another group of trekkers, followed by their porters, passed Fernanda and Randy. A regular parade of Japanese men and women and then natives in red shirts with the expedition company logo, High Adventure. The High Adventure porters carried heavy packs that towered above their heads. Their appearance surprised and puzzled Fernanda, and for a moment she wondered if Pani had hired them as well to find his son. Then she remembered that this was the main Camino Inka, the main trail to Machu Picchu. There must be many such tourist expeditions going on. Later they would leave this trail, and take one much less frequented. The side trail leading to the Wari people.

"Do you think we'll find him?" said Fernanda.

"The boy?" said Randy. "I don't know. We'll give it our best shot. Because this was what you wanted, yes."

"I know," she said. "Maybe I was wrong to get you into this." She drank her last drop of water.

"I've got a little left," said Randy, offering her his bottle.

She drank all he had left as well. And wanted more, but there was no more. Not until lunch.

"What if we find him, and they won't release him to us?" said

Fernanda.

"That's why we brought Big Chance," said a voice behind them. She turned and saw Ed had come back down the trail. "And little Chance," he said, showing them a full size pistol.

"Whoa!" said Randy. "Where, how did you get that?"

"Connections," said Ed. "Mind if I sit with you?" He looked quite tired himself, with his sprouting beard and those dark rings of fatigue round his eyes.

"Do you know how to shoot that thing?" said Fernanda.

Ed laughed. A weary laugh. Fernanda felt sorry for the old man.

"Shall we go on?" asked Randy, getting up.

"No," said Ed. "She'll wait for us. After all we are the paying party."

Randy sat back down. Fernanda reached out and took his hand.

"Ed?" asked Fernanda.

"Yes?"

"Maybe we should go back?"

"Go back?" said Ed.

"You don't look well. And I am so tired."

Ed looked at her with the kindest eyes. "I have to go on," he said. "I'm trying to prove a point to my wife."

"Your wife?" said Randy.

Fernanda and Randy looked at each other.

"Dear Ed," said Fernanda, "didn't you tell us your wife is dead?"

"She's passed away," said Ed, "but I still hear her. At times. Her voice in my head."

"Do you hear her now?" asked Fernanda.

Ed smiled. "No, but I sense her. Near. She wants to say I told you so, but is holding back."

"Told you so what?"

"That the trek would be too much for me."

"She may be right, Ed. You look as tired as I feel," said Randy.

"Oh, we'll break for lunch soon. I'll be okay. I really just wanted to come down and tell you, that if something happens to me, if I become incapacitated, I want you to take the gun."

Fernanda looked how serious Randy got.

"I understand," he said. "You can trust me, Ed."

"Me too," said Fernanda.

Ed's eyes crinkled with an ironic smile.

"You know, I've always wanted to go to Siberia," he said. "People think it is a frozen hell, but in the summer, I've heard you can see mushroom clouds of butterflies, like atomic bombs. Imagine, an atomic bomb of fluttering butterflies."

"Sounds scary and beautiful," said Fernanda.

"I would like to live to see Russia," Ed mused. He stood up like an old man stands, in slow motion. "Let's go get lunch."

They climbed the trail together, moving stiffly, a step behind each other, all three breathing hard. Fernanda wondered if she or Ed would be the first to drop.

19 Lunch, then off the beaten trail

Paro the cook and medicine man, with his fat face and chin whiskers, stood in his apron at the head of the table, proudly showing the trout dish and fat corn kernels as he served up a plate for each of them, along with cups of steaming tea overflowing with coca leaves.

"Wait," said Isabel, holding her fork in the air. "The first bite should go to Pachamama." She cut a bite with her fork and dumped it on the ground. "You see, I am Catholic, but still I respect Pachamama, giving what is due to her."

"To the earth goddess," said Ed, dumping the first piece of his fish on the ground as well.

Chance realized after two quick bites everyone was looking at him. He dumped a small piece of his fish on the ground too. Hopefully Pachamama likes third bites as much as first bites.

The gang at the table gobbled up the food, while the porters, off by themselves, ate a simpler dish.

They sat in a clearing with a mottled sky as their roof, with cloud-shrouded mountains as their walls. A stream running over smooth rocks was their sink, providing water to boil and refill their drinking bottles.

During the meal Kalene told a story about how, in a previous life, she had seduced every single man in the vast Spartan army camped outside Troy, seduced them all in less than a month. Chance sat with his mouth open, his eyes wide, during the entire adult-rated tale.

None of them mentioned the boy, how his time was running out. None of them said what they were thinking, was he even in these mountains? The odds said they were on a wild goose chase. A fool's errand. Chance realized this, but kept the truth to himself.

After the meal Isabel passed out copies of a map, with an X marking the planned campsite for tonight and another X for the Wari settlement. "Just in case we get separated. Note we are here." She showed them on her map as they crowded around. "We will take this turnoff an hour from now, from the main trail. We need to get here." The distance was great. But the names of the mountains and even the line of the trails looked familiar to Chance. He excused himself and took the map she'd given him off a ways, sitting in the shade of a tree with his back to the others. He pulled out his map to the pyrite mine, the one made for him by the girl in Pisac. The map to the mine and the shining path of quartz crystals. What if he returned to the girl in the market after this was all over, walked up to her and dumped fifty pounds of fool's gold right on her table. That would get her attention. Surely then she would forgive him for the other day when he was drunk?

On the other hand Kalene had gone bonkers over the fool's gold he had shown her yesterday afternoon. Over the shiny balls. "I feel like I am holding a missing piece of myself," she had told him. She rolled them in her hands, watching how they sparkled.

"I have other balls," he'd told her. "Softer, snuggled up to a sleeping giant."

"I'm sure you do," she replied, but it was only the pyrite she wanted to hold. He let her keep all she wanted.

Now he was thinking, perhaps he could impress Kalene with a huge specimen directly from the mine? Perhaps he could win her with that offering? If only she didn't give him the heebie jeebies, with her tales of past lives and dead conquests.

Incredible. Chance couldn't believe how well the maps matched up. Like overlapping pieces to the same puzzle. Not to scale of course, but the path names matched here, and here. If he was right, tomorrow morning they would be close to the turnoff that led to the mine. Maybe he could check it out by getting up extra early. Yes, that is what he should do in the morning, check out the validity of Maria's map. See if he could find her mine. After all, he could easily catch up to the others, after checking out the mine, if they left without him. The others walked as fast as three-legged turtles.

20 A history lesson

So they hiked again, single file, like mountain goats, digesting lunch, mindlessly following their leader. Without question or second thought they stepped where she stepped, they paused when she paused, they listened when she spoke. Isabel, the lady from INC. Ed had given up all ideas of leading the expedition himself. In his current shape, exhausted, sweating yet freezing with each blast of mountain air, his head literally killing him, in this shape he was completely at her mercy. When she turned off the main Inca Trail onto an older trail, a less used narrow trail, he did not hesitate. He followed blindly. As did the others.

"The Wari Trail," she called out.

"Will we see a condor?" asked Fernanda.

"When I was a child, on this trail, I always saw condors. Majestic birds, wings spread across the sky. Magical birds. My people say the condors are messengers for the Gods. In the old days, before

Pizarro came with Christianity, the people put small condor statues on their roofs. Blasphemous, the Christian priests said. They made the people replace the condor statues with crosses to represent Christ, between statues of bulls that represent the power of the Spanish empire."

"I noticed those still being used," said Randy. "On the tiled rooftops of a lot of the homes."

"The Spanish priests were expert at converting the people by merging their existing practices and imagery with the practices and imagery of the Catholic Church," she said, stopping to allow everyone to catch up. "Trading one symbology for another."

"For example?" Ed managed to bark from the rear of the parade.

"For example? Well," began Isabel, "for example my people were very religious, thousands of years before the Spanish invaded with their Christianity. We were not godless pagans, as the Spanish claimed. We had our Gods. We met at sacred places, with our priests and our shamans. We held ceremonies, and gave offerings to the Gods, and listened to their wishes. Only, when the Spanish came, they abhorred the thought that we worshipped other Gods. The Catholic Church fanatically destroyed our places of worship. They built Catholic churches on top of our most sacred grounds. In Cuzco they knocked the tops off wonderful Inca buildings, and used the marvelous fitted-stone walls and foundations to build new Spanish styled buildings. When we had the earthquake of 1986 much of the colonial construction was damaged while the original Inca stone walls did not budge, so tightly they fit together, so well they are made. The invaders did not understand that my people knew what they were doing. That the old way, in these lands, was actually better than the new ways of the invaders."

"Like sacrificing children?" said Ed, taking the offensive despite his condition.

"You don't understand, what that meant," she said. "Anyway, my people stopped doing that hundreds of years ago." She glared at Ed over the top of her sharp nose. "Drink and let's move." She did not wait for them to drink. She sped up the path, quickly out of sight.

"A little sensitive on the issue," said Randy.

"I wish I could see a condor," said Fernanda.

"I once flew on the back of a black swan," said Kalene. And as they marched on the Wari Trail, huffing and puffing, she told them a long story that ended with her seducing the entire fearsome guard of the Turkish Emperor. "Their sweat smelled of garlic," she said. "Made me hungry."

21 Campfire Divinations

Fernanda couldn't believe she had made it, to the clearing of the campsite, where they would spend the night. Such a long way up the mountain. So many steps. The porters had already set up several two person tents for the trekkers, and a large dining tent to protect them from the high mountain winds and possible rain. A fire near the dinner tent heated a pan full of white meat and a side dish of boiled potatoes. A stone outhouse, located 20 yards downhill, downwind, was surrounded by a herd of grazing llamas. In the unnatural silence of the mountain clearing, with only the occasional crunch of foot on gravel, as the sun went low and the air turned frosty, Fernanda felt her heart beat. Or was it her baby's heart?

Isabel sent the hikers to their tents, to rest while Paro finished cooking up dinner. Little dishes full of freezing stream water were left at the entrance of each tent, along with wash clothes, for freshening up.

Fernanda and Randy took turns splashing their faces. Once inside their pup tent, Fernanda pulled off her shoes and socks and asked Randy to massage her tired feet. She moaned, the strokes of his hands on her feet felt so good. Strange, she heard someone echoing her moans. In the tent next to theirs. Moans followed by muffled curses. Strange rustling.

"Ed's tent," whispered Randy.

She pulled her socks and shoes back on. Randy followed her as she crawled awkwardly out of the tent.

Fernanda leaned down in front of Ed's closed tent flap. "Are you okay, Ed?"

A deep moan answered her. "Cramps," he said. "Fricking cramps."

"Can we help?"

"Salt and water," he said. "Can you get me salt and water? Oh dammit!"

She heard him thrashing about, but dared not enter the tent without his permission. Instead she and Randy went over to a porter by the fire and asked for salt and water. He said something but they didn't understand a word.

"He speaks only Quechua," said Paro, coming up to them. "I speak four languages."

"Ed is asking for salt and water," said Randy.

"Is he nauseous?" asked Paro. "Does his head hurt?"

"I don't think so," said Fernanda, suddenly feeling a little nauseous herself.

"Good," said Paro. "Not altitude sickness then. You do know that altitude sickness can kill?"

"Walking in the mountains can kill you?" said Fernanda. She had no idea.

"Some are more susceptible than others. The cure is simple enough. You go down."

She realized then what a fool she had been. And how much they were at the mercy of these people they did not even know. By insisting that Randy take on the task of finding little Daniel, she had put all of their lives in danger.

Dios mio, Daniel, where are you? Is there hope for you?

"Here," Paro said to Fernanda, startling her.

He poured salt into her hand, and gave Randy a bottle of water. "We'll boil more after dinner," he said.

"What's that?" asked Kalene, out of nowhere, surprising Fernanda. Her friend pointed to a wrap on the ground next to the food. Some kind of dried plant poked out at the ends of the wrap.

"Ayahuasca plant," said Paro, rubbing his scrubby beard.

"For tonight's divination ceremony."

Kalene held out her hand over the wrapped plant and shook it. Fernanda saw a drop of red, two drops, fall from Kalene's fingers, down onto the Ayahuasca plant.

"Did you cut yourself?" asked Fernanda.

Kalene pulled back her hand, held it up to her face. "Why yes," she said. "I must have pricked my finger." She turned and headed back to her tent.

Dinner was excellent if sparse. A kind of chicken omelet. Fernanda laughed when Chance forgot again to give his first bite to Pachamama. Dessert was a syrupy fruit that Fernanda did not really enjoy but ate anyway. They had a choice of coca leaf or chamomile tea. Fernanda thirsted for a Coke but settled for sweet tea.

"Paro, could you teach me?" asked Fernanda.

"Teach you what?" said Paro.

"Could you teach me how to heal? With herbs?"

Paro smiled, wiggling his chin. Such a peculiar man. "Yes I can teach you what I know of natural healing. But I recommend you go to medical school first."

She wondered why he said that. Was he making fun of her?

Still, she would like to learn what she could from him, if the opportunity arose one day. For natural healing fascinated her. She trusted it so much more than modern doctors and medicine with their expensive drugs full of side effects, effects worse than the disease they was supposed to treat. Randy said Fernanda did not like modern American medicine because she was Mexican, with only Mexican schooling and Mexican superstition to go on, but she knew better. Natural was the way to go. Natural was always better.

The sun had set by the time they left the dining tent, the temperature dropping with it. Fernanda and Randy were halfway to their tent, huddled together, trying to pass warmth to each other, when they heard Isabel call them back.

"Paro is ready for the divination, if you wish. Come to the fire."

Logs had been thrown on the cook fire, turning it into a bonfire, cracking and popping, sparking comets across the black sky. The gang settled in a circle around the fire, on large rocks and fallen logs placed round the fire especially for them. The porters sat on stones just beyond the inner ring. Fernanda stretched out her feet and felt the warmth invade her shoes.

"Not too close," said Ed. "You'll melt the rubber soles."

"Fire scares me," said Fernanda. "But I like the warmth."

"I could almost lie down in it," said Kalene.

"Don't tell me," said Chance. "You did once, in a past life."

"Once or twice," said Kalene. "I remember the last time, a hundred years ago, they lay my body down into a fire at the top rung of the burning ghat in Varanasi."

Fernanda shivered at the mention of the place. Randy's head spun round. "What a strange thing for her to say," he whispered in Fernanda's ear, keeping his eyes on Kalene.

"She is, well, different," was all Fernanda could think to say.

"She looks different, in this light, with her beetle juice war paint on," said Randy. "Kind of . . ." He decided not to say the word apparently, but Fernanda heard it in her head. Evil, thought Fernanda. Why does she look so evil?

Was the light, she realized. The firelight made them all phantasms, ghostly figures, not solid at all. She shivered, but not from the cold wind.

Paro came into that ring of human ghosts, wiggling his whiskers like a fox. Even from this distance Fernanda could see the dilated, bloodshot eyes, could see how he clinched his teeth. How much Aya-what-cha-call-it had he taken? Would he go crazy right in front of them?

"Ask him," said Isabel, sitting on the other side of the fire. "He is in trance. Ask him what you will."

The gang naturally turned to Ed.

"The boy," said Ed. "Will we find him?"

"Yes," said Paro without hesitation.

"Alive?" Ed quickly added.

"You cannot change the question, after asking," said Paro the shaman under trance, said Paro the madman. He jerked his head to the dark wood beyond, then back again. He looked restless, restless. He could not keep his hands still.

"So we are on the right path?" asked Randy.

"Yes. And no," said Paro. He turned to Ed, "Aren't we all dead, the me of a moment ago, the me that answered you and the you that heard my answer? He that answered is dead, but he that answers now is not. He that listened is dead, but he that listens now is not. Do you see? Do you understand? Each step on the path we are someone new. Only the path is continuous."

"He will answer so," said Isabel. "He sees all sides of the question. Up to us to interpret."

The fire popped, making them jump.

"I see you," said Paro. "Without your masks. I see you all clearly." He looked directly at Fernanda. "The soon to be dead and the soon to be born." He did a silly little dance, then focused again. His head began to move in tiny jerks, side to side, side to side, as if he were trying to catch something fleeting with his eyes. Something invisible to the rest of them, some menace swirling around Fernanda. She shivered. She had seen shaman perform before, in Mexico, when she was young, and so she knew that this man, Paro the Wari shaman, was the real thing. Hadn't he just announced that she was pregnant, something he could not have known otherwise. But who was to die? Surely not her? Was she to die on this hike in the Andes?

Paro's face shone, reflecting the churning, whispy flames. The look on his face reminded Fernanda of the dreadful holy men in India. Of the crematorium ghat where a black body burned in superheated flames. Of how they cracked open the skull, while the body still burned, to release the soul. Body to ashes. Ashes to the waters of the Ganges.

"You," Paro shouted, pointing to Randy. "Your heart has two masters. Ha!"

Randy swallowed hard. No one knew about Julie. He hadn't even thought about her since coming to Peru. Before Randy could respond, Paro turned to Chance.

"And you," he said, his whole right arm extended towards Chance. The tattoo of entwined snakes on his forearm seemed to weave in and out. "You are both sides of the coin. But who will flip for you?"

Chance reached into his pocket, to take out a coin, to make a joke of Paro's words, but already the shaman had moved on.

"You carry death," he said to Ed. "Shall I take a look? Shall I fix you?" Shaman Paro held out a small knife. Fernanda had not seen it a second before.

"Give that to me!" ordered Isabel.

Ed stood, reached behind his back, as if to withdraw his weapon.

"I'm just trying to help," Paro said. "An expert trepanning will fix him good."

"Give the knife to me!" Isabel ordered.

Paro reluctantly handed her the knife. Ed sat back down.

He danced then, Paro, danced in slow motion, summoning the power of the herb. Suddenly looking exhausted, he dropped to his knees. Studied Kalene. Shook his head slowly. Looked at all of them, then back at Kalene as if he didn't understand.

"What the hell are you?" he said to her. He held his hands out, half in prayer, half in defense. "You are not from here, and you are not from there. Oh God. Oh Goddess. You are not from anywhere. Am I to be your puppet?"

Everyone looked at Kalene. Isabel stood. Took a step back. This was not going as she expected, Fernanda could tell. The porters leaned in, trying to understand what was happening.

Kalene smiled and shrugged her shoulders. "Do her," she

said, pointing to Fernanda. "Divine her."

Paro looked at Fernanda, back to Kalene. He hesitated, but did as he was told. Studied Fernanda. Took her in. Finally he spoke, wonder evident in his voice. "Love," he said. Fernanda felt her spirits lift at that, until she noticed how his face shifted from joy to sorrow and back again, as quickly as shuffling cards. "You are a vessel overflowing with love," he pronounced. "I've never seen a more perfect offering." He repeated his words in Spanish, "*Ella es amor puro. Es el sacrificio perfecto.*" Then in Quechua. For all to hear.

He turned to Isabel, then to Kalene. Had to shield his eyes, as if Kalene shone too brightly. "I understand," he barked at her, blinking rapidly, spit flying from his mouth. "I understand what you want from us, now."

They all looked at Kalene.

"You understand what?" asked Isabel.

"What does he understand?" said Fernanda, squeezing Randy's hand, looking to her young friend Kalene. "I want to go," she said aloud. "I don't like it here anymore. It's not safe. He's not safe!"

"He's stoned," said Randy. "He's stoned out of his mind."

Fernanda felt a cold drop from the sky splash on the top of her head. She looked up into nothing but a black emptiness, a promise of what was to come. The fire dimmed.

"We're here for a reason," said Ed, straightening up. "Don't forget that. We're here to save the boy."

"We won't find him," said Fernanda. "Not alive. You heard Paro. *Todo esto es un desastre.*"

"She's tired," said Randy. "Come on, let's go." He helped Fernanda to her feet.

"Wait," said Kalene. "Ask him what is going to happen tonight."

"Tonight?" said Chance. "What is going to happen tonight?"

"Paro, tell us," said Isabel, taking a wary step towards him. "What is going to happen? Tell me how she knows!"

Paro slowly lay himself down. So close to the flames Fernanda could see the brown skin of his hands heating to red as he stared into the fire. His black eyes watered, full of flame. "I don't want to see," he said. "I'm tired."

"Tell us," said Isabel.

"Please," said Fernanda.

Paro whimpered. "Tonight. Tonight I see that one of us will die. Die from a kiss."

"Oh hell," said Ed. "I've had enough of this." He got up and stormed away. The others followed, tired and confused. What kind of a divination was that? Pure insanity.

"Was he speaking poetic, just now?" said Chance. "That last thing he said. About tonight. Does he mean someone is going to have sex?"

"I think so," said Kalene.

"How did you know he was going to say that?"

She winked at him.

They retreated to their tents, while Isabel, back at the fire circle, yelled at Paro in Quechua, and he mumbled something back. Fernanda wondered what she was telling him, what he was telling her in response, as she crawled on all fours into her tent. Then the cramps started, to Fernanda this time. She cried out in pain and began to massage madly her calves, and then her thighs, as the terrible, powerful attacker inside her legs moved upwards. What can you do when your own body is assaulting you? She wreathed as distended shadow figures on the tent wall danced in rhythm to the spasms in her legs. Randy climbed in and tried to help. Until his own calf muscles locked up, putting him on his back. This trip was beginning to feel to Fernanda too much like their disastrous stay in India.

They drank water and eventually, if they were careful how they moved, their leg muscles loosened and stopped cramping. They stretched out in their sleeping bags, afraid to move after that.

Fernanda had witnessed tonight incredible things, things that filled her with wonder. And fear. And a longing, wrapped up in her fear, to do a divination herself. To peer into her own heart, to know her destiny. Why did everything have to be so menacing, so unclear? Why couldn't one just know one's fate, and prepare for it?

At least she had Randy. Randy her rock. Her poor obedient rock.

"Randy?" she whispered.

"Hmm?" he answered in his sleepy voice.

"*Lo siento.*"

"You're sorry? Sorry for what?"

"Shhh," she said. "I'm sorry for, everything. For putting everyone in danger. Let's turn around tomorrow. Let's go back down."

She heard him struggle in his bag, heard him turn towards her. "Damn!" he said. He had another cramp. Massaged it as he whispered.

"But I thought you wanted me to help find the boy."

"Daniel's not on this mountain, Randy," she said in a low voice.

Silence.

"Listen, Fernanda. We're half way to the Wari settlement. Doesn't make sense to turn around. I think you're just tired. Let's wait for morning to see if you still feel the same way."

Fernanda started to cry, silently. A sure sign that she was overtired.

"OK," she managed to say to him. But it wasn't OK. She wasn't OK.

After a few minutes, in the uneasy comfort of their tent, in the confines of her sleeping bag, all zipped up, near Randy but not close enough to feel his warmth, uncertainty fell over Fernanda like a spell. What did the shaman Paro mean when he said Randy's heart had two masters? Should she worry? She almost woke Randy, to tell him her big secret, that she was pregnant with his child. That her fear of losing the baby on this hike, losing his baby, was the reason she wanted to go back. But that wasn't true. She was pregnant yes, but the main reason she wanted to go back down was that she was scared. Scared for all of them. Scared of something she sensed in that thin mountain air that barely filled her lungs, every breath of which left her feeling cheated. She turned and turned, the wrinkles in the sleeping bag pinching her back until finally, gratefully, she slept.

22 The weight of the world on Isabel

In the large tent, they sat close, facing each other, Isabel and Paro, both of them shaking, but for different reasons. Paro's nervous system was still at the mercy of the herb, while Isabel was shaking from the contradictory emotions caused by Paro's suggestion. Based on his divination of the Mexican woman, of Fernanda, they both realized that she was special. They talked in Quechua about this, in low voices, so as not to be understood by the Americans in nearby tents.

"Paro, for three years now, since my husband died and I took over as leader of the Wari people, you have been my right hand man."

Paro nodded.

"Once before you suggested I let a sacrifice take place. Once before I listened to you. When the elders had that beautiful little girl stolen from Cuzco. I had been tribe leader only a few months, unsure of myself. I turned to you for advice. You remember what you said to me then?"

"I told you the ground beneath your leadership was shaky. That it was too soon to take on the elders over the issue of human sacrifice."

"You told me to listen to the arguments of the elders, how it was far better to sacrifice one, than for all to suffer. Better to give to the Inti a precious offering, than to risk the wrath of Apu. Apu, whose vengeful earthquakes and avalanches could slaughter thousands."

"I told you what I held to be true," said Paro. "The same as today when I tell that I have never seen a more perfect specimen to be sacrificed than Fernanda. She was born to be an offering. I swear to you. Her death, done right, could appease the Gods for a thousand years. She would make the perfect last human sacrifice of our people. For all people."

"I did not want to kill the girl then," Isabel said. "I do not want to kill this woman now."

"Let our people have one last great sacrifice," he suggested. "And no more."

"The same promise. One last time," said Isabel. "I'm afraid, Paro. Afraid the people will ignore me, no matter what I say. You realize the porters heard you, when you were in trance. They may take matters into their own hands."

"I believe you should listen to your people's wishes," said Paro. "Trust in our traditions."

"I'll think about it," she said, and left his tent for her own.

Three years ago she gave in on the subject. Gave in to the insistence of the elders, to the divinations of Paro, to the reading of the intestines of three sacrificed llamas. She told them they could march the child to the summit, to her death, as long as they promised that this would be the last one. The final sacrifice. Three years ago.

And Isabel did nothing as they fed the girl chicha and sweetened corn mash, did nothing as they fattened her for the Gods. She never tried to stop them as they took the girl and carried her to the summit and placed her like a ball in the snow, with a miniature brass llama cupped in her tiny hands. Isabel let them leave the child on the mountain top, shivering in her womb of snow, fingering the llama charm, wondering when her mommy was coming. Mommy who would take her in her arms and warm her. Mommy, who did not come, as the girl's fingers turned blue. Mommy, who never came, as the shivering stopped and the little girl's, the poor little baby's, eyes froze shut.

Three years ago. Isabel let them. And hated herself now for doing so.

23 Kalene slips up

Kalene lay on her back in her unzipped sleeping bag, smiling at how well the divination had gone. She listened as cold drops exploded on her tent walls, the night rain calling to her. Calling for her to join the night. To join the unnamed horrors that come out at night, in the mountains, in the cities, horrors that come out everywhere, at the setting of the sun. Horrors that stalked men and women, and tore them apart. Time for her to act like one. Time for her to choose. A man. Tonight. She rose up on an elbow. Her breath steamed in the cold crowded space of the tent. Kalene rose to her knees and undressed quiet as a mouse, left the tent quiet as a bird. A mere flapping of the flap of the tent. The falling rain hid the noise of her bare feet striking the puddles. Rain coursed over her bare back, down her arms and legs, made her feel chillingly alive.

When she touched his cheek, and he opened his sleepy eyes, she could see he thought she was a dream. "Miqual," she said, calling him by his name. "Quiet," she told him in Quechua, one of the myriad languages she spoke. He opened his mouth, startled by this naked woman leaning over him, dripping on him, but she put a finger to his lips. She could tell from his eyes how her touch there inflamed him, how his blood was already running to his nethers. To his *palo*. "Come with me," she whispered. "I need you."

He followed her, unquestioning, out into the cold rain. "What do you want from me, Goddess?" he asked, the rain striking the side of his face, running down his neck, under the collar of his shirt. "What can I give you?"

"Teach me how to fall in love," she told him. "And I will spare you."

"I will, I promise," he told her, gripping her by the arms, pulling her close.

But already, as he pressed himself against her, as she removed his pants, she knew the hollow of his promise. And after they mated, on the grass, after he mixed his rain with hers, and the shower stopped, and the insects and toads in the forest came out from hiding and sang their lonely whistles and scritches and croaks, she lay there on her back and felt nothing. Absolutely nothing in her heart towards him. She reached over, touched his forehead, and put him to sleep. She did not bother to fight the need she felt then, the compulsion that had driven her for a thousand years. She did not try to stop her inner craving. She licked her lips and moved down his front, slowly, like a big cat, parted his legs, sniffed his deflated member, and bit off his balls.

24 One chance meeting after another

In the confines of his tent, in the light thrown from his flashlight, Chance sprayed droplets of cologne on his sweat-soaked clothes, sneezed twice, and waited for Kalene's visit. He even thought he heard her stirring in her tent at one point, after the rain started, but she did not come to him and eventually he fell into a fitful sleep.

The sun had yet to rise when Chance woke, remembering his plan to check out Maria's map. To see if he could find the path of shining crystals and locate the pyrite mine. But first he had to pee.

Luckily for him the rain had stopped. He tried to make little noise as he unzipped the tent flap slowly and climbed on all fours outside into the night. The cold air made him regret not bringing his jacket. The flesh of his hands and face complained. He reached the stone outhouse, a spooky place at night. He left the door open to the stall, and peed like a horse, the yellow liquid frothing and steaming where he missed the hole.

For some reason he thought of his son, little one year old

Chip, and he smiled. His wife Crystal came to mind as well, which turned his smile sideways.

A sound behind him. He whirled around, his penis dangling in front of him.

"Oh," said Kalene.

Chance stuck his penis in his pants. "You?"

"Sorry, but girls have to pee too, you know."

"Where is your flashlight?"

She pointed to the full moon shrouded by thinning clouds. As he left the stall, she passed by him, pulled down her pants and squatted over the hole. Right in front of him.

Doubly embarrassed, he looked away.

"Cold this morning," she said.

He could hear her tinkling. "Yes," he said. "I thought you might come to my tent last night." He faced her when the tinkling stopped.

"And there I was waiting all night in my tent for you!" she said, standing, pulling up her panties and her pants.

Chance focused his light on her face. Gave her a good hard look. Was she playing with him? Making fun of him? He noticed a cat-like glint in her eyes, a crimson smear from her mouth to her jaw.

"You still have some of that beetle juice on your face," he told her.

She wiped around her mouth. "I'm free, now, if you want," she said, reaching to take his hand, but he dodged her touch.

"I have something I need to do this morning."

"In the dark? No one else is even up," she said.

"Remember that pyrite I gave you?"

"The balls of fool's gold? Of course I remember. It was only the day before yesterday."

"Seems so long ago," said Chance. "Anyway, I have a map to the mine. The pyrite mine. I think it is close by. I am going to search for it before the others are up."

"Can I come?" she asked, skipping up beside him. "I've never felt so attracted to rocks before."

"No," he told her. "I have to move fast."

"Please," she said. "I assure you I can keep up."

Darn if he didn't believe her. And damn if he didn't want her to come. She was a pretty young thing, after all. "Do you promise you'll do as I say?"

"I promise."

"Then get your stuff, quietly, and meet me on the trail in 10 minutes."

He went to his tent and packed. He had very little water and no food. That was a concern. But he only planned to be gone a couple of hours. He took out a piece of paper he had in his pack and wrote a note for Randy and the rest. He wrote that he and Kalene were going to search for a pyrite mine close by, but should be back soon. He checked his watch. 5:10 am. "If not back by 9 am," he wrote, "go on without us. We'll catch up." On the back of the note he sketched a copy of the map Maria had drawn for him.

Kalene was standing outside his tent when he crawled out, waiting like a puppy for its master. Like one of those excited puppies that bite you when you least expect it. He swore if she had a tail it would be wagging. He decided not to use his light. The moon was bright. He found a rock and placed the note on the table in the dining tent. Turned and ran smack into Kalene. "Please," he whispered. "Not so close."

They set off at a fast pace, Kalene matching his every step. He switched on his flashlight. The trail looked eerie at night, in the artificial glow. Thin fog tendrils reaching out from the brush, like a creature looking to feed. He found the turnoff to the mine, based on his map and the distance they had covered. A tight squeeze, hardly a trail at all. Kalene followed behind him without complaint. They hiked rapidly as the sky continued to lighten. Reached the spot where the trail should have become shiny, but no such luck.

Chance took them a ways farther up the trail, searching this way and that. Still no luck. No quartz trail at all. He finally gave up and sat down in a huff. Kalene plopped next to him.

"Can't find the path of shining crystal," said Chance. He took the last sip of his water. Kalene drank the last of hers. "The shining path that leads to the pyrite mine."

"Should we go back, then?" said Kalene.

Chance checked his watch. 8:05 am. They would be late, getting back, already. "I guess. We might as well." He stood up, only to notice they were not alone. They were surrounded by a small army. Native people in worn-out military fatigues surrounded them. Youngsters. Kids. They held old rifles and pistols too large for their hands.

"*Quienes son ustedes?*" asked Kalene in perfect Spanish.

"Who are *you?*" asked a tall man entering the path. He had ribbons and metals on his green shirt and an officer's pistol hanging from his belt. His green beret had a condor insignia. His face hid behind a full beard.

"We are prospectors," said Chance, handing the commander his map. "We are looking for a shining path that leads to a mine of fool's gold."

"Because you are a fool?" said the man. He looked at the map and began to laugh out loud. He passed the map to his young lieutenants, explained something to them. They all laughed themselves.

"*Pirite*," said Kalene.

"*Unos tontos*," Chance heard more than one of them say.

"Where is your support team?"

"You're looking at her, general," said Chance, indicating Kalene.

Kalene smiled at the commander.

"Our tent is down trail a ways," said Chance. "We are prospectors."

"Not anymore," said the commander of the gunmen. "You are now prisoners of the soldiers of the Shining Path Communist Movement."

"The Shining Path?" said Chance. Vaguely, vaguely, in the back of his mind, he remembered hearing something about them. He'd been so obsessed with crystals for years now, he'd naturally assumed a shining path would be, well, crystal. Quartz crystal. He realized the joke was on him.

"Oh my," said Kalene, rubbing her hands together.

25 Ed's worst nightmare

Fernanda stands over Ed, in his dream. She leans down, slowly, lovingly, and kisses him right on the mouth.

He tries to move his arms but he is restrained.

In Fernanda's right hand are shears, the kind herdsmen use to clip the wool from their sheep.

Ed realizes his pants are down. She places the cold steel shears across his thighs. He tries to move his legs but those too are constrained.

"Trust me," she tells him, opening the shears, placing the blades on each side of his testicles.

He woke with a start, his t-shirt soaked. At first he thought it was sweat, then he realized the tent roof had leaked in on him, onto his bag. He cursed and sat up.

The light of the sun glowed through the sides of his tent. He could hear the others stirring, could smell ham frying and coffee brewing. Another day hike to the Wari settlement. Surely he could make that. If only his head didn't hurt so badly. He dried off and put on dry clothes. Crawled out the tent and down to the outhouse to take a shit. He forgot toilet paper. Frick it! He used his underwear as best he could, then threw it in the corner. Returned to the tent for a clean pair.

Just then the alarm went out. A porter yelling in Quechua. Another. He grabbed his gun, slipped it in the back of his pants, just in case. He climbed out of the tent.

"Ed, please come," said Isabel. "Something is wrong."

A porter was missing. Unheard of. Porters don't go missing. Not her porters. "Something is wrong," she repeated. She called out the porter's name.

"Do you know anything about this?" she asked Paro, standing over the breakfast fire, wearing an apron.

"Don't ask me," he said. "I slept like the dead."

"Tell the others to search," said Isabel, "while you serve breakfast."

Randy and Fernanda came into the dining tent right after Ed, who picked up the note from the table and sat down.

"Oh hell no," he said. He passed the note to Randy.

Fernanda read over his shoulder. "He's gone off with Kalene? To search for fool's gold?"

"Typical of Chance," said Randy. "Thinking only of himself."

"Maybe they took the porter with them," said Ed. "To not get lost." He told Isabel as much when she came in with Paro and the food. Mango pancakes with a side of ham.

They discussed the possibility as they ate. Ed had never expected such exquisite food on a mountain trek. The pain in his head eased a bit.

Sure, that was what happened to the porter, they decided. He went off with Chance and Kalene.

They had just finished their meal and were enjoying coffee when Randy broached the subject of their turning around.

"Isabel, Fernanda told me last night that she really wants to go back down. That she isn't comfortable continuing to the village."

"I," started Fernanda. "I think maybe you should go on Ed. If you are up to it. But the rest of us, Randy, Kalene, Chance, and me, I think we should go home."

Ed felt a knot in his stomach. The pain in his head got worse, just like that, at the thought that he now had to decide between following the woman he had been assigned to by INTERPOL, or blow off INTERPOL and his career and save a little lost boy. Maybe save a little lost boy. Probably not save a little lost boy.

Can't make up your mind, can you?

Shut up!

You knew it would come to this. You knew you'd have to decide.

Shut up I said!

"I wish you would go on with us," said Isabel. "We have a grand celebration planned."

A yell, outside the tent. Almost a scream.

They ran out, Ed leading the way into a brilliant morning sun. He had to shade his eyes for a moment. Made out one of their porters standing by the stone outhouse. The porter waved them down. They jogged that way together, through a soggy field covered with pellets of llama manure.

Even Ed was shocked by what they saw lying there behind the outhouse. Even Ed, who'd seen unspeakable things in his long career with the FBI, working in one of the most violent countries in the world. Working in America.

The poor guy had bled out, it was evident, even though the rain had washed most of the blood away. Had cleaned him. Only a splotch of dark red left on his bare legs, but they could all see the jagged tear in his ball sack.

"He's been neutered," said Randy.

"*Si*," said Paro.

"Is this what you predicted last night?" asked Isabel.

"I don't know," he told her. "I don't know what I meant."

"Where are his testicles?" asked Fernanda.

"As if you didn't know," said Ed. His head pounded. He felt nauseous. The earth beneath his feet was not firm. He reached behind his back and drew his gun. Pointed the hefty piece at Fernanda's stomach.

"What are you doing?" asked Randy. "Ed why do you have a gun on my wife?"

"Fernanda I arrest you," said Ed. "In the name of, in the name of..."

"Are you insane?" said Isabel. "This was a big cat attack. Caught him with his pants down."

"You have the right, the right to remain," said Ed. How his head pounded. "I am an FBI raging." What, what was he saying? His head swam. Shallow water. His wife wanted to tell him something. "Not now!" he yelled.

"What?"

"Not her first kill," Ed told them. "A half dosing. A doozling." His vision blurred. "In India."

"Oh frigging India again," said Randy. "Has Kalene been telling you stories? Fernanda didn't even want to go there. Put the gun down, Ed."

Ed's vision blurred. Not now, he pleaded. Not before I arrest the woman and find the missing boy. But Fate waits for no one, you know that, his wife told him. He tried to keep hold of the gun. What gun? He held no gun. Somewhere on the ground. Must be. He leaned over to see, only to fall into a galaxy of black stars.

26 Prisoners of the Shining Path

Chance sat cross-legged on the straw, his legs chained together. The straw smelled of goat poo. Llama poo? Was not a bad smell actually. Kind of homey. He lifted his wrist to see the time, only to remember they'd stolen his watch. The little devils. He guessed it was noon. Were they not going to feed him and Kalene?

A few yards away Kalene sat, her legs chained as well. Before them sat two kids playing soldier with real rifles. Rifles pointed at Chance and Kalene.

"If they try to escape, shoot them," their commander had said.

"I have money, at home, to pay our ransom," Chance had told him.

"You'd better hope your friends can get to it, then." And he left them in the barn with the two baby guards.

Chance wasn't stupid enough to tell the commander that his friends were only two or three miles away, on the Wari trail. Wouldn't do him or them any good. No, he'd have to get word back to his wife Crystal, in Arkansas. She should be able to raise $20,000 or so. Sell one of the machines, a backhoe, if she had to.

As far as Kalene, he knew little about her but assumed she came from money. Maybe she could get enough from her relatives for the two of them.

The door to the barn opened and the commander came back in. He tossed a stone gently towards Chance, who caught it and by its heft, before he even opened his hand, knew that it was a chunk of fool's gold. Sparkling, heavy as real gold, with perfect square crystals. Not malleable like gold though, brittle as a woman's heart.

"You spoke true," said the commander. "There is a new mine up there. Exactly where your map indicated. The miner is long gone. Frightened off by us, I suppose. Still, I would like to know where you got this map."

"I bought it," said Chance. Something told him not to tell the truth.

"From whom?"

"A taxi driver. In Cuzco."

"His name?"

"Didn't get his name," said Chance. "Drove a black sedan. With those colored taxi indicators on the side."

"A taxi driver drew this map for you?"

Chance nodded, as nonchalantly as he could.

"Lunch!" cried the commander over his shoulder.

Plates of roasted corn kernels and boiled potatoes were brought in. The commander sat on the straw, between the two of them, as the plates were handed out. A filthy little boy, no more than six, handed them dirty plastic cups of water.

Chance pinched a roasted corn kernel from his plate, and dropped it to the ground. "For Pachamama," he said.

The young guards' eyes went wide.

"How dare you insult me," said the commander. "How long must my people suffer from the opiate of religion? How long must we bow down to distorted images of our Creator?"

"I'm sorry. I wanted to show respect."

"Communists don't believe in any religion," said Kalene.

"How do you know that?" asked Chance.

"How do you not know that?" said Kalene.

"The Shining Path *is* our religion," said the commander. "Enlightenment, freedom from government leaders dictating our lives, leaders that profess to know what God wants us to do. Claiming that they are descendants of God, or God's favored sons. It's not that we don't believe in the Creator, it's that we don't believe that others know more about God's wishes, based on their inflated egos or the reading of old books, than we do ourselves. We who sit on God's shoulders, here in the Andes."

"Sounds about right," said Chance. He picked up the roasted corn he had dropped on the straw, and put it in his mouth. "To Pacha-me," he said between his teeth. To his surprise, they all laughed. Kalene, the commander, the young guards.

Maybe he could deal with these people, thought Chance. By connecting with them. Common goals. Maybe going through the Shining Path was the best way to reach the pyrite mine after all? To get at the fool's gold and all the riches it could bring to an entrepreneur like himself?

"I hear you and I respect you, sir," said Chance. "Damn priests and religious fanatics. God doesn't need interpreters. He speaks with the taste of roasted corn. With the thirst-quenching power of chicha. By the way, do you have any?"

"No," said the commander. "Not for you. Not for enemies."

"Ah, commander, today's enemy is tomorrow's pal. Look at the Americans and the Japanese. The French and the Germans. Commerce, general, the possibility to make Dollars, Yen, Francs, and Peruvian Sols, that's what brings enemies to toast each other with pitchers of beer. That's what's going to make us the best of friends."

The commander eyed Chance a good while, nodding slowly, sizing him up.

"We shall see," he said finally. He got up and left.

Randy then turned his silver tongue on the young guards.

"Do you speak English?" Randy asked them.

One nodded. The other said, "*Un poco*. A little."

"Kalene once rode on the back of a black swan. Big black bird, like your condor," he told them. "Wait, now that I remember, it was a condor! The biggest you could ever see." He nudged Kalene with his foot. "Tell them about it, Kalene. PG-13 version, please. Or maybe PG-10?"

She began the telling, with much animation. The youngsters sat down, lay their rifles across their laps, and listened with wide eyes.

27 Trepanage

Ed awoke atop the dining table, wrapped in blankets. He could not move his arms. Ropes, at his wrists. He could feel the bonds tighten when he struggled against them. He tried to move his head but it too was secured to the table. How his head pounded!

A blur of a woman's face came into view. He could not see clearly. "Isabel?" he asked. The pain behind his right eye was blinding.

"No," she said. "I am Fernanda."

"You are under arrest," he told her.

"Ed, you are ill," she said. "You have a tumor. Paro told us. He says tumors make people imagine things."

"Like that dead man? I imagined him lying there, his eyes and mouth open, his . . ."

"No," said Fernanda. "The porter is dead. Some big cat, says Isabel. Or," and here she hesitated, "Ed, Paro said maybe the tumor made you hallucinate. And in your hallucination you killed the porter."

"No. No not I. You are the cat," he told her. "Not a bird at all. Blah blah blue." What was that he just said? Form the words, Ed. Concentrate. "I am not hallucinating. I am an agent assigned to tail clue."

He swore he saw tears in Fernanda's eyes. Do mass murderers cry? Could the pain he felt actually be killing him?

"Ed the tumor doesn't let you think straight. You are a lonely retired private detective. You told us so yourself. You like to birdwatch. That's all you want to do anymore. That's who you are. That's why you came to Peru. To watch birds."

"True," he told her, "la la la lue." He had meant to say, "You were the bird." But words were hard to form now. He tried again to lift his arms. The weight of the world held them down.

"Have him drink this," he heard his wife say. My wife? Where had she come from? They tried to pour a nasty liquid into his mouth. He spit most of it out.

"Again," his wife said. Why was she so insistent? They closed his nose and he had to swallow so he could breathe again. He coughed, and swore at them.

Paro came into view, with his soccer ball of a face with whiskers like tufts of grass. The crazy medicine man held what looked like a corkscrew.

"Rabba rue," Ed told Paro, though it made no sense, not even to Ed.

How Ed's head pounded, with every heartbeat. Yet from far away he could sense a tsunami coming. A wave to take him out to sea.

"I'm going to remove the tumor," Paro told him. "Before the poison spreads. Before you lose your body as well as your mind." With a corkscrew? What kind of joke is this? I must be dreaming. I never went to Peru. I must be in a coma in a hospital in the States. He tried to remember who he was and why he was where he was, but the incoming wave washed over him then and it didn't matter. Nothing mattered. Only the riptide, and the gulls overhead, and the taste of salt on his tongue. Or was it blood?

"On the table!"

"Are you sure you know what you are doing?"

"I know the blood flow in his brain is restricted and

he will suffer brain damage or worse if I don't operate immediately."

"Oh my God no, don't."

"It's all right. Take her out of here."

"You can't just. . ."

"Out!"

"No, sorry, I can help."

"Then hold his head. You others hold his arms."

Grunts and moans and will it ever stop will it ever stop will it ever?

28 Who is that boy?

Chance amazed Kalene. The way nothing seemed to faze him. The way he could talk his way out of anything. The Gods smiled on Chance, it seemed.

"I like being trapped here," he told her. "Trapped with you."

"You make me smile," she told him. "I like that. I think I'm beginning to like you."

"When we get out of here, maybe . . ."

"You are best to stay away from me, Chance. I bite."

"I'm sure you do. That's what interests me most about you. Your pearly whites. That and the sense of danger I feel whenever you get close."

A charmer, he was. Natural born. Would be his

downfall.

"So you are afraid of me?" she asked.

"Should I be?"

"I told you so."

"Ah, so you did. I wasn't listening, I suppose. I rarely do. To warnings. About what not to do."

Kalene laughed. He delighted her. She wanted that second to devour him with her kisses, but the chains kept him at arms' length.

Hours passed. The two prisoners of war shared their outlook on life, and laughed together at their hardships. Kalene swore she felt something blooming in her heart for him. She was sure of it. A kind of warmth whenever he neared her, a kind of desire to get nearer whenever he spoke. She wished it was true, anyway. Just like Fernanda had done at one time, just like Fernanda before her, she wanted so to fall in love with Chance. But wait, Fernanda had never fallen in love with Chance. She'd only lived with him. Randy was the one Fernanda loved. With all her heart. This wasn't what she wanted after all, Kalene realized. Not Chance. He would fail her, like all the others, for he was a flawed lover, at best. Or was she the one that was flawed?

Still there was something about Chance. His carefree

style and his pyrite. That wonderful sparkling stone from the mine. From her mine. Already she claimed it.

The commander returned, a sparkle in his eye.

"I will show you the mine," he said. "I want to know if you think it has value."

"Of course the mine has value, dear commander," said Chance, rising, rattling his chains. "Why else do you think we risked our lives to come looking for it?" The commander unlocked them from the posts, but left the chains on their hands and their feet.

They walked out of the barn, slowly, awkwardly, and up a small path.

"There's money to be made in pyrite crystals," said Chance, shuffling along in his chains. "And I know how to mine them."

"We can mine the pyrite ourselves," said the commander.

"All the better," said Chance. "And I will pay top wholesale dollar for what you mine."

In front of the small entrance to the mine, near a spring, was a simple foot-powered polishing machine. That was where someone had polished the rough stone into smooth balls crossed with veins of pure sparkle.

"Blood pyrite," said Kalene in a low voice.

"What?" said Chance.

"Nothing." She suddenly felt a kind of nostalgia, a homesickness, a longing for something that had been taken from her. The pyrite? That made no sense. Why would she feel so strongly about a particular stone? Not even a precious stone, at that. She could barely contain herself though as they walked into the granite space. It's calling to me. Calling to me. The scars on the walls showed where the miner had ripped out rock to get at the vein.

"This is a new mine," said Chance. "They haven't yet taken much pyrite at all."

Chance ran his hands inside a large crack in the wall. He looked about and spotted a tool on the ground. "May I?" he asked. "This is a nice vug full of crystal."

"Go ahead," said the commander, his hand on his pistol.

Chance reached into the vug with the tool and pried off a large cube of pyrite. Just as the cube came free, Kalene screamed in pain. She jumped on Chance, pulling him away from the wall.

"What is it?" said Chance.

"*Que pasa?*" asked the commander. The young guards pointed their rifles at the prisoners.

"That hurt," said Kalene. "When you did that. When you chiseled off the stone. That hurt me here." She pointed to her chest.

Chance gave the old, "she's crazy" sign language to the others.

"Aren't all women?" said the commander.

They left the mine, the commander and Chance haggling over details of their partnership all the way back to the encampment. As discussed, the Shining Path would mine the pyrite. Chance told the commander there could be a half million dollars of mineral in the mine, if marketed correctly. That he would pay ten US dollars per kilo of the rough stone, twenty US per kilo for stone that had been polished into balls. Chance would also cover shipping to the States. The commander told Chance that they could communicate through a PO Box in Cuzco. One that he already used.

Happy at the prospect of easy riches for his cause, the commander had his men remove the chains on Chance and Kalene, and invited them to afternoon tea before he let them go.

"We have a special guest that I would like you to meet," he told Chance. "She may be the one communicating with you on my behalf. In our dealings."

"Sure," said Chance. "But then Kalene and I really must head out. We've got so much to do on our side to get this rolling. Logistics, you know. Got to tidy up the logistics."

"You know I think you are a little crazy," said the commander. He rubbed his beard, a half smile showing. "But so am I. For haven't I spent half my life chasing an impossible dream? The dream of equitable existence, of shared wealth. I fear it is just outside my reach, this dream of mine."

"Things not going so good?" asked Chance.

"The people don't like change. Even change for the better, it seems."

"Well, all we can do is try."

Two long wooden tables were arranged outside for all to sit. Chance counted eight kids, with guns, sitting down. Boys and girls. A few teenagers as well. Four grown armed men sat by the commander, with three unarmed women standing behind them.

From the low ranch house stepped another young woman in a too tight wool sweater and a western style skirt.

Beside her walked a little boy carrying mail on a silver platter. He was the same six year old that had brought them water when they were still chained up in the barn. Only now the boy's face was clean, and he wore a fresh shirt.

"Chance," whispered Kalene. "Who is that little boy? He looks so familiar."

Chance turned pale. But he wasn't looking at the boy, he was looking at the young lady heading straight for them.

"My daughter Maria, up from Pisac," said the commander. "I would like you to meet our new business partners, Maria. Chance and Kalene."

Kalene stood up while Chance fell off his seat.

29 Decisions, decisions

Randy paced the dining tent, Ed's heavy gun stuck in his belt. The tent smelled of alcohol and something indeterminate. Body fluids? Fernanda sat at the table, where Ed lay face up, a pool of congealing blood around his head. A head now heavily bandaged around his right eye. Fernanda held Ed's hand. His fingers twitched every so often, as if he were dreaming. She hoped it was a pleasant dream.

"I think he will recover," said Paro, returning from washing up at the stream. "A nasty tumor though, one of the worst I have removed. Right on his optic nerve, pressing on his brain."

"Did you have to go through his eye?" said Fernanda.

"Yes," said Paro. "Don't worry, they make excellent glass eyes in Lima."

"How the heck did you know what he had?" said Randy.

"I saw the disease in him last night, during our ceremony. Remember? The spirit of the Ayahuasca filled me like never before."

He checked Ed's pulse. "As far as the surgery I performed, I have been taking care of my people for years. Surgery is a skill passed down to all shamans," said Paro, rubbing warmth back into his hands. "My father taught me. His father taught him. And yes, well, I guess I should credit my years of medical school as well."

"You're a doctor? Not a shaman?"

"I am a doctor *and* a shaman," he said. "A surgeon, too, when the need arises." He gave her a wink.

"But did you have to go through his eye?" repeated Fernanda.

"The point of least resistance," said Paro.

They stood together, looking at the slow rise and fall of Ed's chest.

"How long before he can be moved?" said Fernanda.

"Oh he can be moved any time," said Paro. "Infection is our only concern at this point. Isabel sent a porter running to bring aid from our people. To bring others, tonight, to carry him to the settlement. Where he can be properly cared for."

"Wouldn't it be better to take him to town?" said Randy. "He could come down with Fernanda and me and the rest."

"No, he is my responsibility now," said Paro. "And I am going up, not down."

"When is the solstice celebration?" asked Fernanda.

"Tomorrow," Paro said. "Don't worry, I don't think they will start the sacrifices without us."

"Sacrifices?" said Fernanda. "I thought you said . . ."

"The llamas," said Paro.

"They sacrifice llamas," explained Randy, drawing up to Fernanda, putting an arm around her shoulders. "They cut up white llamas and pregnant ones. They consider them most special. I read about it on the computer, when I was researching."

Fernanda felt sick. All that she had seen last night and this morning, and only now, with Randy's words, did she feel sick.

She dropped Ed's hand and hurried outside the tent. She bent over and vomited breakfast. I must tell him, she thought. Why haven't I told him about the baby?

They had lunch down by the stream. Boiled potatoes with greens.

"Why haven't they come back?" asked Fernanda. "Why haven't Chance and Kalene returned? I want to go home."

"I don't know," said Randy. "Maybe they got lost."

"What if that animal . . .?"

"Don't think such things," said Randy. "They are fine. I am sure."

"Should we go look for them?"

"And get lost too?"

"No, I mean take a porter with us. To help us find them." Fernanda's hands shook ever so slightly. These had been two trying days.

"I'll ask Isabel if she can loan us a porter."

30 Of All the Dames

Chance smiled weakly at a frowning Kalene as they sat again, in chains, on the straw that smelled of goat and llama, in the barn of the encampment of the Shining Path guerillas.

Maria hadn't meant to do them ill, Chance was sure of it, but her reaction at seeing him at the table, and his falling stupidly off his chair, his reaction at seeing her, well, even a dullard like her father the commander could put two and two together. These two especially.

"You drew him a map," shouted her father, "with our position marked right on it?"

"I was drunk," she told him.

"He got you drunk!"

Chance shook his head. He was in for it now.

"Chain them," her father commanded. "Chain them and throw them back in the barn. And you my daughter, you are prohibited from leaving the ranch until further notice."

"But father, I have my job in Pisac!"

"You will be one of us from now on. Live and die with us. Think about that the next time you are tempted to let a man get you drunk. Think about that the next time you are asked to draw a map!"

"Did you notice the boy?" asked Kalene. "I almost called out his name."

"What name?"

"You know. Daniel."

"You're telling me we found Daniel? The boy everyone is looking for? The purpose of this almighty historic trek? But he's not supposed to be here. He's supposed to be at the Wari village, isn't he? No one is going to sacrifice him here."

"Oh, he'll be sacrificed all right," said Kalene. "As soon as the soldiers find this place and shoot everyone in sight."

"Well," said Chance. "I'll be damned. So she knew about the boy and didn't tell me."

"Who knew?"

"Maria. Like the general said, I kind of got her drunk. And just before we left the restaurant there in Pisac, I showed her Daniel's picture. And she played dumb. She lied to me."

"Maybe she doesn't come up to visit her father very often," said Kalene. "Remember Daniel has only been missing a few weeks."

"Maybe she is the one who took him," said Chance.

He spat on the straw, studied the chains that fastened the two of them to a center pole in the building. He was sure he could cut through the pole, using the rough edge of the chain, given enough time. Given a few days.

31 Isabel makes a stand

"I will allow no such thing," said Isabel. "First you want to go up with us to my settlement, so I arrange this, despite what you suspect of my people. Then after one day of hiking you tell me you want to go back down, that this is all a mistake. And now you say you want to go off searching for your friends, who had no business going off by themselves. I won't hear anymore nonsense. We will all wait this day for them to return. Wait together."

"You don't understand," said Randy. "Chance is my best friend. Our oldest friend."

"And Kalene is my . . . newest friend," added Fernanda.

"You must wait until morning, when I have reinforcements from the settlement. Men with weapons to protect us against whatever it is that killed my porter."

She ordered the tents moved into a semi-circle at the entrance to the dining tent, where Ed lay recovering. Two men on guard, in turns, all night.

They ate only crackers and cheese for dinner. Fernanda hoped the chamomile tea would calm her nerves. The Andes were worse than India, she decided.

"There's nothing we can do for them tonight," said Randy, outstretched in the tent with Fernanda. "Best to try to sleep."

"I know," she said. "I hope when we wake they are back. Chance is such an idiot."

"He is," said Randy. "A lovable idiot, though, if there ever was one."

Fernanda leaned her forehead against Randy's. They sat like that a long while, as if sharing secret thoughts.

"'I'm pregnant," she said.

"I wondered," said Randy. "Your breasts are larger, and you have a bit of a tummy."

"So you knew?"

"I wondered, that's all."

"And?"

"I think it's great. I've told you before. I think we are ready."

"I hope I am," said Fernanda.

He kissed her lips. They lay back in their sleeping bags, her hand in his.

"Are we going to find them, Randy? Chance, Kalene, the boy?"

"I hope so," he said. "If the mountains will give them up." He reached and felt for the gun, to be sure where to find it if trouble arrived in the night.

32 Chance has a dream

In Chance's dream a goat is standing in the straw next to the chained Kalene.

"I know you," she tells the goat. "You are Lord Hanuman's goat, the all-devouring."

The goat says nothing.

"What has that old Monkey God been up to?"

The goat just looks at her.

"I'm not going back. Not yet. I must know how it feels to be in love. I must!"

The goat turns its head.

"You would deny me this!? Me, the Great Kali, the Dark One, the Devourer of not just things but Time itself?"

The goat does not reply. But it does disappear.

A hand on Chance's shoulder. He half opens his eyes, pushes the hand away.

"It's me," the figure above him whispers. "Maria."

Chance popped up, as did Kalene.

Next to Maria stood a second shadow. A little shadow.

"Daniel?" Kalene whispered. "Are you Daniel?"

"I am soldier," he whispered back. "I follow her," he said, indicating Maria. He gave Chance a salute. Chance saluted right back.

Maria unlocked their chains. "I did not know," she said. "I swear I did not know my father he was stealing the childrens. I thought the boy he was some street boy." She led them to the barn door, pointed behind the building. "I guess he has lost so many soldiers, my father, that he has taken to stealing the childrens from Cuzco to fill his ranks."

In the light of the moon, Chance caught a clear view of her face and read the sincerity there. Clearly. Still . . .

"How do we know we won't be shot as soon as we step outside?"

She drew close to Chance, whispered in his ear so the boy

could not hear. "My father insists that I join them," she told him. "My father who kills people. Innocent people. I could never be one of them. I thought he was dead until a few weeks ago. I hoped that he was dead, my father. Then I saw him return to our place with his childrens."

She pushed the door open a bit more.

"This way, quick, there are no guards this way."

"I am sleepy," said Daniel.

"He will carry you," said Maria.

"Sure," whispered Chance. He lifted the boy atop his broad shoulders, and off they went with him across the way, towards the shadows of the woods.

Maria led the way. She forced a new trail through the brush, slowly, as quietly as she could. Only with distance and time did they speed up.

When they had covered perhaps a mile, they found a trail and broke into a jog, downhill, almost tripping several times. Once Maria thought it was safe, she slowed and began to talk to them in a low voice. She explained that the pyrite deposit was a discovery of hers actually, the previous year. Two years had passed, at the time, since she'd had word from her father, off fighting in the mountains to the north. She worked the mine herself off and on, until her father returned with his troops and she had to stop. Felt it was better to stop. Why did her father have to come back?

"I was fine, living my life alone," she told them. "Mother died when I was born. Father raised me, in his way. Taught me to raise myself." She glanced back at them, making sure Chance still had the boy. "I stay in Pisac, with a friend, selling my pyrite in the market to the tourists Thursday through Sunday. People from all over the world. Everyone loves my pyrite. As much as Chance, even. And some tourist men, they try to love me, just like Chance."

Chance cleared his throat. "I'm sorry about that. Your beauty clouded my better judgement."

"Hush," she told him. "Every other week I make the hike to my father's place, to mine the pyrite and to turn some with my polish wheel to crystal balls. Before he comes back, my father, and he ruins everything for me. I will not join his army. I will be free of him."

"You are a brave girl, Maria," said Kalene. "Thank you."

"Yeah thanks," said Chance. "For saving us."

"I am not saving you, no, Mr Chance" she told him. "I would never do that. I am simply using your legs, your manly strength, to save the boy."

"Ah," he said.

"How *is* Daniel?" asked Kalene.

"He sleeps."

Another half hour and she had them back on the main Wari trail. They rested five minutes, then hiked until they came upon the Wari encampment. Two native men sat by the fire. Maria started to steer them around the camp.

"It's okay," Chance said. "These are our friends."

Maria studied the porters standing guard. "Those are Wari," she said. "I don't trust Wari."

"Neither do I," said Kalene.

Chance looked from one to the other, confused. "But I recognize those porters. I recognize the camp, too, though they've moved the tents around. Randy and Fernanda must be here, I'm sure of it."

Maria bit her lower lip. "Father will come this way with his soldiers in the morning, looking for us. We must warn these people. Even the Wari should be warned. That they need to move on." She walked towards the porters guarding the camp, with Kalene behind her and Chance hauling the boy. "Ho," she said, getting their attention. Then she spoke to them in Quechua.

"Remember us?" said Chance. "Friends." He handed the boy over to the first guard's outstretched arms.

33 Friends?

Fernanda came running from the darkness into the fire light. Threw herself into Chance's arms. "Oh Chance! We were so worried. And the boy? Is that really Daniel?" She turned to Randy strolling up behind her. "Randy, it is really Daniel?"

The boy looked at them with round eyes from his perch in a porter's arms, looking like a speechless owl.

"Yes, it *is* Daniel," said Kalene. Fernanda gave her a hug as well.

"I am soldier," he told them, rubbing his eyes. "*Soldado del Sendero Luminoso.* You are my prisoners."

Chance laughed. "Yes we are," he told the boy.

Isabel came out from her tent, looking angry. Then she saw the boy and her expression changed to one of great concern. "Daniel! Godson!" She ran up and hugged him.

"The Shining Path had him," said Chance.

"The guerillas?" said Isabel. "I don't understand. You visited the Shining Path? How did you possibly get him away? How did you escape yourselves from those blood-thirsty people?"

"Maria helped us," said Kalene. "She was a captive too."

Maria looked at Kalene, who simply smiled back.

"You must break camp," Maria told Isabel. "For they will follow. Soon. We must head down to safety."

Isabel yelled some commands to the porters in Quechua. She turned back to Maria and the gang. "I have men coming from our settlement atop the mountain. They are already near. Men with guns. The safer route is up to meet them."

"No," said Maria. "We are better to leave everything here. And run down. Back to civilization. My fa . . . they will not follow us there."

"I want to go down too," said Fernanda. "But we can't leave everything, dear. We have a very ill man in the tent."

"Who?" asked Chance.

"Ed. He fell ill this morning and Paro had to operate."

"Operate?" said Chance. "What the hell have you guys been up to? I leave for a few hours and you start playing hospital?"

"There's more, Chance," said Randy. "One of the porters was killed last night. We don't know by what."

"Killed?" Chance thought about that but it made no sense. "Killed by Shining Path guerillas?"

"We think it was an animal. Caught him when he was peeing."

"Oh great," said Chance. "I got to watch out for my dongle now when I take a pee in the woods?"

"Probably a jaguar," said Isabel. "But that's not our present concern. The Shining Path are who we need to worry about. Unpredictable, dangerous men."

"As are the Waris," Maria whispered to Fernanda. Fernanda could tell she was making an uneasy partnership. That she preferred for them to simply make a run down the mountain. Fernanda preferred that route as well. But then Maria said, "Okay. I agree. If you have men coming to help, we can head up to meet them. But we have to leave now! Travel light. Carry nothing but the sick man. And Daniel."

They made a stretcher for Ed, and in less than twenty minutes they were headed up the Wari trail, Daniel riding snug on Chance's back while two porters carried Ed. Every so often, as they trekked skyward, toward the dawning sun, Ed would wake and cry out, "Edith! Edith!" Call out for his dead wife. Perhaps, this high in the Andes, this close to Heaven, she would hear, come down, and give him comfort.

34 The Calvary were Indians themselves

Randy heard gun shots. He was sure. Far away, but scary none the less.

"They're shooting up our camp," said Paro. "They will know we headed up. No more resting. No more stops. It is now a race to the top."

Fernanda huffed and puffed, trying her best to keep up. But she couldn't. She couldn't go on.

"I can't, Randy. Please, go on without me."

He would hear none of that. He make her climb on his back, and he carried her a good half hour, giving her a chance to rest, but at the same time burning out his own legs.

"Stop, rest," Isabel told them.

"We mustn't," countered Paro.

"Look at them," she said, indicating Randy and Fernanda, Ed

and the boy.

Paro shook his head.

They scattered out on rock ledges and boulders. Paro passed around two bottles of water, the only water they had.

"Are they so bad?" asked Fernanda. "Would they really hurt us?"

"People who believe that what they do is more important than life," said Maria, "these are the most dangerous."

Ahead, on the path, people running down. Isabel waved. They waved back. A dozen men, running with reckless abandon, holding spears and clubs and hunting rifles. The cavalry had arrived. Hurray for the cavalry!

Isabel had a powwow with them, then and there. Randy watched how they stuffed their mouths with coca leaves. Isabel reached out, indicating Fernanda, Ed on the stretcher, and the boy. Pointed them out to the newcomers. Six of the men dropped their weapons and jogged down to the gang. Four of them picked up Daniel and Ed and started immediately up the path. The two remaining men went to pick up Fernanda.

"No!" she said. "Randy?"

He made a snap judgment. "Let them, Fernanda." His own legs were giving out. He couldn't carry her again if he wanted. These

Wari men appeared to be young and strong and used to climbing. He nodded for them to take her.

They lifted Fernanda, and like supernatural beings they sped up the trail they had just raced down for hours.

Fernanda looked back, from their arms, fear in her eyes.

"It'll be alright," Randy called after her. But he had to wonder. This wasn't as bad as India, no - with every passing minute it seemed to be getting ten times worse.

"Let's go, everyone," said Isabel. "If we don't stop again we can reach the safety of the settlement by noon."

Another rifle shot. Maybe three miles back.

"Out of the frying pan, into the fire," said Kalene. She scampered closely behind Chance, up the worn stone steps. The ancient steps where white men once chased after natives.

Randy, way in the back of the pack, was struck by the realization that when Isabel had requested help from the Wari settlement, when she had sent her runner to get assistance, it was because of the dead porter. Not because they were under threat of attack from Shining Path guerillas. So why had so many Wari warriors come running down to meet them? That wasn't logical. If Randy prided himself on anything, it was his ability to grasp the logic in a situation. Did Isabel know Shining Path guerillas were near, is that why she asked for so many armed men to come? Or was there another reason? He strived to catch a glimpse of Fernanda who he'd allowed to be carried off by the warriors, but his dear wife, his one love, was long since gone.

ELSE

Part Three: The Final Sacrifice

ELSE

35 Isabel prepares for a fight

Her people streamed from the settlement like ants from a threatened mound. Everyone afoot, in leather sandals, fathers dashing with sacks of potatoes, water jugs and weapons, mothers hauling babies in slings on their backs or pulling toddlers by the hand.

"Evacuate!" Isabel cried again in Quechua, Isabel from INC, Isabel the leader of the Wari people. "To the ruins!"

To the Inca ruins above the settlement. Where the enormous stone walls could stop bullets. Where the single narrow entrance leading to the ruins would allow for easy defense. As in the old days.

"Evacuate!" Isabel cried still, waving them on. She couldn't believe the series of events in the past few days, events had started out with small promise, developed into something of tremendous promise, only to turn dark and confusing. She had inadvertently brought danger upon her people, and for that she cursed herself.

Back in Cuzco, at the hotel, she had jumped at the chance to show these meddling foreigners that her people did not have the missing boy. Too, she had looked forward to the trek to her settlement as a welcome chance to participate in the tribe's ceremony, the traditional sacrifice of the white llama and a guinea pig feast. Yes, there was the slitting of the throats and gutting of the animals for divinations, and these traditions would repulse the foreigners. But they would prove too that her people were no longer slaughtering little boys and girls. Not that they ever did – for you don't slaughter your prize children, you lead them to the snows atop the mountain to be taken by Inti, the great sun God, or Mama Killa, the Goddess of the moon.

But even that kind of sacrifice they no longer did. Thanks to Isabel. As the Wari leader upon her husband's death, she had put an end to the practice of child sacrifice.

But then Paro's divinations around the campfire seemed to demand a sacrifice. The sacrifice of Fernanda. Isabel had never seen Paro so transformed. So sure of his declarations, so full of godly power. He was convinced, and managed to largely convince Isabel as well, that Fernanda was the ideal vessel to carry her peoples' wishes to the Gods. That her body, her spirit, would make for their perfect final human sacrifice.

As ruler of the Wari people, a people who knew better than anyone how the Gods demanded sacrifice, Isabel was hard put not to follow up on such a divination. Here, before her, as if delivered by the Gods, was a woman so full of love that her soul cried out to be taken. So much love! In one woman! She must be sacrificed!

Normally Isabel had no stomach for human sacrifice. She wondered why she felt such a strong pull now to see Fernanda killed? She had been so set against any more sacrifices of this nature. But she had been greatly moved at the divination, almost as if under the spell of the herb herself.

But what about the attack on her porter? A conflicting sign. That was no cat who tore into him. That was the work of a demon.

And the missing boy! Dear Daniel. Her godson. Appearing out of nowhere. Brought to camp by that hulking Chance. That was no coincidence. The Gods were speaking, but the message seemed jumbled at best. Did they bring Danial to me, the leader of the Wari, for me to sacrifice him? Sacrifice my own godson? Was that their message? She must sacrifice the two of them, Fernanda and the boy? For the good of the world? Why? Why must she do that? Yet how could she not do the will of the Gods? How could she disobey them? She must do her duty. And yet. And yet.

She would have to make the decision, but not now. First Isabel had to deal with these Shining Path idiots. Once a powerful, feared army, the movement had dwindled down after battles and desertions, to scattered groups of children led by fanatics. Dangerous fanatics who killed without mercy. Without understanding the horror in the act of killing a fellow human when it was not for the glory of the Gods.

"To the ruins!" she called out, noticing the Americans just now plodding into the settlement with the last of her men. "There's safety in the ruins."

36 But where's Fernanda?

"Where's Fernanda?" Randy yelled after Isabel, on the path from the settlement to the ruins just above.

"Can't you see all is chaos?" Isabel snapped at him. "She's probably up there already."

Randy, Chance, Kalene and Maria stayed together as they followed after Isabel and the Wari clan. They all funneled up a stone staircase through a narrow doorway in a thick wall of polished, fitted boulders. Men with rifles and machetes and what looked like large slingshots lined the path, ready to stop any comers.

Passing the guards the gang followed Isabel into a large stone building with a missing roof. Most of the Wari had gathered there. Randy noticed Ed on a straw mound along one wall. Paro was kneeling by his head, treating him with an herb compress.

"Have you seen Fernanda? I can't find her," said Randy.

"No. Last I saw she was with the boy."

"Where?"

"In the crowd, coming up here. I'm sure she's fine."

"How is he?" asked Randy.

"Why do you look so far away?" asked Ed, starring up at Randy with one eye.

Randy was surprised to see Ed awake. He lay under a beautifully woven alpaca wool blanket.

"You've lost your perspective," said Paro.

"Ha!" said Ed, his lone eye looking at Paro. "You're telling me!"

Ed looked back at Randy. "This madman shaman was just explaining to me that he is indeed a licensed surgeon." Ed tried to get up, but Paro stopped him.

"Lay still."

"Also his grandfather taught his father who taught him," said Randy. Kalene and Maria came over as well.

"Which is true," said Paro. "I mix the knowledge of the old with the new. Best of both worlds."

"I have to admit my previous pain is gone," said Ed. "But now it feels like someone yanked my eye out."

"Scooped out," said Paro. "To the objection of your friends.

But I had to. The tumor was on the optic nerve. Cutting off blood flow."

"How did you know?" asked Randy.

"Divination," said Paro. "Intuition. Years of healing. Chance."

"I had nothing to do with it," said Chance. "I was out looking for the mine."

"Have you seen Fernanda?" Randy asked Chance.

"I haven't seen her."

"Is it true about the boy?" said Ed. "Did you find him? Is he safe?"

"Sort of," said Chance.

"I can't believe I was so wrong," said Ed. "That it was the Shining Path who had him all along."

"But now he's gone missing," said Randy, "Again. Along with Fernanda."

"Fernanda?" said Ed. "Are you sure she did not take the boy herself? Are you sure she's not a killer?"

"Of course she's not a killer! What is it with you on that subject?" said Randy. "Isabel's men came down to camp and carried Fernanda and Daniel off just as the Shining Path guerrillas approached. And I haven't seen either of them since."

"Sorry, no, I suppose my perspective was off long before I lost my eye. Strange. Things just don't add up when it comes to your wife. And now you say she's missing?" Ed forced himself up onto his elbow, over Paro's objections.

"I can't find her anywhere," said Randy. "Isabel said she doesn't know. Maybe they were ambushed by the Shining Path? Maybe she has been kidnapped along with Daniel."

"I don't like it," said Ed. "When is the solstice?"

"Tomorrow," said Paro. "Tomorrow we sacrifice the llama."

"And that's all?" asked Ed.

Before Paro could reply, shots rang out, echoing about the walls of the building, making them all lower their heads and cover their ears.

37 A long night

After the echoes of the first exchange of gunfire faded, after the sun set, the Wari in the ruin with no roof built fires to ward off the chill. Potatoes shaped like gnarly fingers were roasted in the ashes of the fires, and handed out as supper. No more shots sounded but everyone remained tense, as long as the smoke from the Shining Path camp could be seen rising to the sky, obscuring, with the smoke of their own fires, the endless spill of stars.

Hours passed. Only the children and the old slept. Everyone else sat red-eyed, staring into the flames. They knew how serious the situation was. They'd all heard the stories of whole settlements being slaughtered by the Shining Path for perceived slights.

The gang, including Maria, had settled around Ed, who slept a while but then woke with a start.

"The Shining Path!" he shouted. "It must be them. They have taken back the boy. And Fernanda to boot!"

"You think so?" asked Randy.

"I, I had a dream."

"Oh," said Randy.

"You think they want a trade?" asked Maria. "Fernanda for me?"

"I think it's possible," said Ed.

"Is that why they are still here?" asked Chance. "Is that why they won't leave?"

"I don't know," said Maria. "I know my father is mad at me. I think he's come mostly for me. Listen, I'll go down and talk with him. If he has Fernanda and the boy, I'll get him to let them go."

"Why would he do that?" asked Chance.

"Because I am his daughter," said Maria. "I will leave with him and do as he wishes as long as he sets them free."

"I don't think it's going to be that easy," said Chance.

"No," said Kalene. "I think Chance and I should go with you, to force his hand."

"Well," said Chance. "I wasn't suggesting…"

"Sure you were," said Kalene. "If we have to, we will sacrifice our lives for Fernanda."

"I never said..." started Chance again, but already Maria and Kalene were off, so he followed reluctantly after them.

Randy tried to join but Maria stopped him. "No, as few as possible. For he may take you all hostage."

"Then no one goes," said Randy.

"Listen to her," said Ed. "It's a good plan."

"What's a good plan?" asked Isabel, coming over after seeing all the commotion on their side of the large room. Maria explained to her in Quechua her plan. "Ok," said Isabel. "But only you go," she said in English.

"And me," insisted Kalene. "Your father can't hurt me. He wouldn't dare."

Isabel stared at this puzzling woman, so full of confidence and apparent knowledge of things she couldn't possibly know the first thing about. "Sure," said Isabel. "You go too." And I hope they shoot that smirk off your face.

38 Kidnapped

Fernanda did not understand why they did not stop at the settlement, why they did not stop at least at the ruins. Where were they taking her and Daniel? And why?

She tried asking the men who hauled her and the boy, men who never seemed to tire. Men intent on finishing their assigned duty. But they spoke neither Spanish nor English apparently.

Finally, after dark, they stopped at a high mountain hut made of dried mud bricks, on the edge of a snow bank. Straw spilled out from the wood eaves.

Inside the hut Fernanda was told to sit with the boy on a hard mat.

"I'm hungry," said Daniel. Fernanda admired the stoic look in his little face. Must have learned to hide his feelings during his stay with the Shining Path.

A fire was lit in the primitive chimney. They offered Fernanda llama meat jerky, but she declined. Daniel chewed a bite of it. Water was brought to them in a llama skin bag – tasted of leather.

"Where is everyone else?" she asked. "Why am I here?"

The leader grunted something she did not understand. She tried to read meaning from his eyes but their expression was dense, untelling.

"I am going to look for the others," she said, getting up. They sat her back down.

So it was like that. They had taken her. For purpose unknown. Or did she know? Could they possibly mean to . . ., no she couldn't let herself think such a thing.

Still, what had Kat said? The Wari sacrificed children. At solstice. Had sacrificed Kat's daughter only a few years ago. The Wari sacrificed *people*. Her recurring dream came back to her. The one that told her she was a chosen one. For some reason she wore the mark of death.

Randy, where are you, my love? Help me. Save me.

She lay down next to the boy and covered them both with a threadbare blanket that only reached her knees. She should get some sleep. Tomorrow she might need all her strength to escape.

39 A shot in the dark

Maria and Kalene walked down the steps past the guard who'd been instructed to allow them passage.

"Father!" Maria called out in Spanish. "Let's talk."

She heard whispers from the tree-line, not far. She called out again.

Her father's deep voice replied. "Come here, then."

"I'm coming with a friend."

"I don't give a damn who you come with."

Maria led the way in the moonlight, Kalene on her heels.

"It will be alright," Kalene told her. "I won't let anything happen to you."

Maria gave Kalene a look. Kalene smiled back. She was having a great time. She hadn't learned what it was like to fall in love yet, but she had really been enjoying playing human with Randy and Fernanda. On this grand adventure that promised human sacrifice and more.

Shining Path soldiers escorted them beyond the trees to a primitive encampment. Maria's father sat down before the fire. He picked up a stick with an impaled, roasted guinea pig. Indicated to the girls they could help themselves as well.

"Do you have Daniel?" asked Maria, sitting across from the fire, declining the offer of the blackened thing on a stick. Kalene remained standing. She could feel the eyes on her and the pointed rifles. She wanted to burst out laughing. Children. Children with guns.

"Who?" said her father, tearing off a chunk of meat with his teeth.

"You know who. The boy you stole."

"How could I possibly have him when you stole him from me?"

"And Fernanda? Where is Fernanda?"

"Who the hell is Fernanda?" her father said, his voice rising, his eyes widening, catching the flamelight. He flung down his meal on a stick. Rose to his full height, pulling his shoulders back and sticking his chest out. "Take her," he ordered, pointing to his daughter. And moving slowly, deliberately, he pointed to Kalene and said, "Shoot this bitch."

A muzzle flared, thunder sounded as a bullet launched towards Kalene's left breast. But before it could reach her, before it could tear through her flesh and bury its hot body inside her rib cage, seeking out her heart, everything stopped. Time. The world. The taking of each breath, the beating of each heart. It all stopped. Even the flames paused. Maria's father's mouth stayed open from his last command, his body in half step.

Puzzled, because this was not of her doing, Kalene struggled to move out of the path of the bullet. But she could not move and barely could she think.

A goat appeared just beyond the fire. After the goat appeared a monkey the size of a man, a monkey dressed as a man, but in royal robes, standing on his hind legs. A monkey man with a fierce intelligent look.

Kalene recognized him at once. Her companion for thousands of years, Lord Hanuman, son of the wind, father of thunder. Hanuman who could lift a mountain, Hanuman who could drink the sea.

"Kali, what have you been up to?" his voice rang out, melodious, firm. He chided her like an older brother.

"Just playing," she managed to tell him, her jaw muscles barely obeying.

"The truth?"

"I told your goat before," she said. "I want to know what love feels like."

Lord Hanuman shook his head.

"For so many years," she continued, "for so many centuries I have reaped the chosen ones, those full of love. I sacrificed them according to God's will. But now I want to know what is so special about love that you have to suffer because of it."

"You don't want to know," he told her.

"She does," said the goat, the great devourer, Lord Hanuman's other companion.

"Let her speak for herself," Lord Hanuman said. All the while the world stood still, the bullet hurling towards her yet at the same time stopped in mid-air.

"Why can't I feel?" she said to her longtime friend. "It's as if I have no heart."

"You don't," said Lord Hanuman, walking over to his goat, petting the beast's sturdy back. "I had to take your heart away from you 500 years ago. I'm sorry."

"You took my heart? I don't remember that."

"When I took your heart I had to take also the memories clinging to it like a starfish devouring a nautilus."

"Why? Why would you take my heart, Lord Hanuman?"

"Why indeed, why indeed." And while the world waited, with all the creatures in the world holding their breath, Lord Hanuman began the story of how Kali the Terrible lost her heart.

40 What love feels like

In the epoch of empire, when kings still ruled and craved gold to squander on their whims and their wars, Kali the Black Goddess grew bored watching over the river Ganga and the inhabitants who lived on her shores. She decided to be reborn, in a faraway place, on top of the new world. In a place that one day would be called Peru.

Her simple parents, living in the high Andes, had never seen such a beautiful child. They named her Sisa, royal flower. Fame of her beauty and smiling demeanor spread over the land as she grew to the age of ten, always helpful, always loving. And though Sisa would miss her parents, she accepted the great honor that was bestowed on her when the Incas came and took her to the capital to be one of the Aklya Kona, the Virgins of the Sun. For only the most healthy, the most beautiful, only those most deserving were taken into the royal house and taught the skills that would make them worthy of being a wife to an Inca prince one day. Or to serve as a royal sacrifice to the Gods.

From the age of ten to fifteen, Sisa spent her days being schooled on the art of weaving fine alpaca wool into caps, sweaters, eventually into blankets with florid designs. She was taught how to chew ground corn in such a way as to infuse the greatest amount of her saliva, then to spit it into the container from which they would make chicha for the royal family to drink. She was taught to cook, not just potatoes and corn but meat as well, for the royals liked to feed often on llama and guinea pig. And yes, too, she was taught, with drawings in the dirt, how to give a man the most pleasure before allowing him to finish. Because even if she wasn't chosen to be a wife to bear children for her king, she could always be chosen to be his concubine.

Her clothes were fine material, her hair combed by servants. She painted her lips with crimson beetle juice, her eyelids with coal. In her free time she liked to go to the quarry and watch the boys and men work the stone. She ate fresh corn and potatoes, and rarely felt sick or even troubled. A wonderful life, little Sisa had. A life that promised the world.

When the Coya Pasca, the high priestess, came to her and told her to prepare to be married, her happiness overflowed. She danced and danced. Could she ask for more?

Her prince, Tupi, was not handsome, but a fine man and kind spirited. He treated her with respect. Made love to her gently, the first time, and only later, when she asked, did he put his entire weight on her, did he exhaust himself and her with his pounding, with his thrusts.

The first child was a girl. Usqui. The cutest brightest thing. Always playing house and telling stories to her imaginary friends.

The second child was Erli, a fine strong boy. He would certainly lead his people to glory one day.

They moved from the capital, up into the Andes, where Tupi would command his own tribe. A beautiful place, where fresh water ran in streams through rain forest. Where everything grew and flourished.

Sisa liked to sit by the stream with Tupi and her children, watch how the clear water flowed over the stones, like love over one's heart. For her heart *was* overflowing. She beamed with love. For her son, for her daughter, for her husband. For life itself. Everyone who saw her recognized this, even worshiped her, in their way, for obviously she was a chosen one. A blessed one.

Rumors came from the capital. Fearful rumors. Invaders from another world. Sisa knew worry for the first time in her life. How could she protect her family?

Sickness came. Horrible coughing and pus bumps. Spots and weakness. Fever as never the shamans had seen. Unknown diseases from an unknown land.

Her people began to die. A few. Then hundreds. Any who treated the sick also died. News from the capital came that many of their strongest warriors were falling ill. Messengers brought the news on the Inca Trail to all corners of the empire, then fell sick themselves and died passing on their message of woe. What horrible plague had befallen her people? And how was it spreading?

The leaders slaughtered their best llamas, selected the most beautiful Virgins and took them to the mountain tops. They begged the condors to take their cry for help to the Gods. But no relief was forthcoming. The Gods went mute. Inti silent. Mama Killa silent. Mama Pacha turned a deaf ear.

Sisa waited and watched as friends died.

Then one day little Usqui did not want to get up from her covers. Sisa touched her burning forehead. Removed the covers, her little nightshirt, and saw the red bumps. As if she been stung by a thousand wasps. A shaman was called, the only one left in their village. He refused to touch the child and was put to death.

Her daughter, her wonderful Usqui, died in Sisa's arms. Such horrible, meaningless loss. Sisa could barely stand the pain of such loss.

Her son Erli fell sick. No, this can't be happening, thought Sisa. How can such happiness turn to sorrow? She begged her husband, her prince Tupi, to do something. To save their son. He sacrificed half their flock of llamas. The boy recovered. Thank God. A short respite from sorrow, though, as Tupi was called away to battle. To fight off the invaders, with his slingshot and pouch of polished stones. Fight off horrid men, if men they were, riding giant skinned llamas and killing with firestick stings, and, as Sisa had become so aware, men who brought with them sickness that knew little cure. Their God was a merciless God. Bow down or be slaughtered, was their God's creed. Or was it, bow down AND be slaughtered.

Sisa got the news a week later. Tupi and most of the men from their village had been killed or captured by the invaders. She had to know which had befallen her husband. Leaving Erli with his aunt, she set off for the capital. Walked down the long winding trail of stone steps, walked the Inca Trail for a week with little food and water, until she reached the capital city. Exhausted, but driven to find her husband.

She stopped short. Bodies. Along the road. A pile of bodies. Some marked with disease, others with wounds of war. The wind turned, and the stench overwhelmed her. Still she wondered if she should dig through the dead, in search of her husband. No, something told her he was still alive, so she left the dead to the dogs and the flies, and pushed on into the city.

Down she walked into the city center, to the enormous plaza. And she saw the first of them. Men, yes, but wearing worked stone that reflected the sun into her eyes. They walked in rhythm, as if they were driven by a single mind. Another invader appeared riding one of the giant llamas Sisa had heard about. What a strange powerful beast was that llama-thing. Large enough to carry a man. Two men even.

She recognized what must be their firesticks, but could not see where they carried their disease. Well hidden on their bodies to be sure.

She went to market, at least that part of life had not changed. Not as many people as she expected, but still life appeared to be carrying on. She asked about the invaders. What was it they wanted? "The mineral used to make the masks for the mummies of our ancestors," she was told. "Gold" they called it. "Are they fools?" she said. "Don't they know it has no value?" "They are fools," she was told. "And demons and worshippers of another God. They will skin you alive if you do not say you love their God." "I love all Gods worthy of love," she told them.

She asked about the captives, where they were kept. She knew the place. Had played in the terrace just in front when still a Virgin.

She seduced a guard, he was, after all, only a man, and stole the key. She hid on the side of the building all night, waiting for her chance to free her husband. But at daybreak many invaders came on the giant llamas. They dismounted and finding the key missing they burst open the door. The leaders of her people, the best and the brightest, the strongest and those most brave, were led out into the plaza, hands tied behind their backs.

Tupi. She saw her beloved Tupi. He held his head high. She started to show herself, then stepped back. She did not want to upset him with her presence.

The captives were led by the invaders to a stone bench, where a man waited with an enormous ax. Sisa watched in horror as the invaders spoke accusing words with their terrible tongue, then marched one of the captives to the stone bench, held the man down, with his head sticking over the edge of the bench, and the giant ax came down.

No! No. They were going to kill them all.

And Tupi was next.

Sisa could not hold herself back. She ran towards Tupi, calling his name. He turned his head, struggled with the men holding him down. He called to her. "Sisa, my love. Look how they shed our blood."

The ax came down.

Sisa half-stumbled, her heart bursting. The Goddess dormant inside her came to life, if only for a second. She hurled the large key in her hand with such strength and speed it flew straight through the right eye of the man with the ax, and drove deep into his brain. He let out a groan and fell backwards, dead.

Everyone stopped and looked at her. Sisa, standing out of breath, no more thought as to what to do. Where to go.

The invaders had seen clearly what she had done, but none could believe. A key? She'd thrown a key from thirty feet and killed as if she had thrown a knife?

"A witch!" the word went out. "Catch her before she kills again."

They took her, roughly, and wrapped her in chains, tied her to a post. They fired arrows point blank into her body. Left her out in the open, in the plaza, for all to see what happens to witches.

She drooped motionless. No more tears to shed. Oblivious to the pain of her wounds. All night she was still, thinking how her love had turned to sorrow, her sorrow to hate. She would kill them all, she decided.

"She hasn't died?" the newcomers asked themselves the next morning, giving her a kick.

They slit her wrists and the veins in her legs. The blood flowed like streams in the mountains, though steaming hot.

The next morning, they poked her and when she moved, they asked themselves again, "She still hasn't died?"

They poured molten lead into her wounds, hoping the torturous pain would scare her soul away.

The next morning, though looking like death, she was not dead. They struck her, and she laughed.

"Fire," they said. "We must burn her."

They piled wood up around her and all day and into the night they burned her body. They could hear her laughter in the flames, as she planned to kill not only the invaders but all mankind. In a moment, as soon as she gathered her strength, she would rise as Kali the Terrible and rip the world apart.

That's when I appeared to her, to Sisa, in the flames.

"Let go, Sisa," I told her. I told you.

"No," you said. "I am gathering my strength, and once I do I shall destroy this awful planet. I shall flood the earth with my spit."

"Let go, Sisa," I told you again.

"I am no longer Sisa. She was weak. I am Kali the Snipper. The Dark Force. I am gathering my strength."

Then I saw inside you, I touched you, here, and knew your heart was in ruins. Not just the heart of the human Sisa, but the heart of a Goddess, of Kali herself. What folly this had been. Your desire to feel love. What folly it is still.

I reached in and gripped your heart with its strangling memories of love lost, and I ripped it from you. I flung your broken heart far away, to the mountains, where it embedded itself into the side of Apu as a crystalline vein of fool's gold. So Sisa could die, and Kali live. But live on without the ruinous memories of Sisa.

Lord Hanuman finished his tale, looked into the eyes of his beloved Kali, and asked. "Do you still want to know what love feels like?"

Kali looked long into the eyes of this strange companion of hers, this man-monkey she'd been with for thousands, perhaps millions of years, so many years that she had lost count.

"I know now what love feels like," she told him. "I love you."

"She loves you," said the goat.

Lord Hanuman blinked and the world spun again, the hearts of all the living beat, and Kalene's heart, the one pierced by a Shining Path bullet, stopped as she fell to the ground, dead.

41 Daybreak finds Fernanda

The men were arguing. Fernanda did not know why. "Solstice." She heard the word Solstice.

"Don't kill us," she told them. "*No nos matan.*"

They ignored her. Probably did not understand. Served Daniel and her a strange mash for breakfast, a strange drink. Chicha? But much stronger. She spit it out. They forced her to drink more. And more still.

They fed the same to the boy.

Cold outside. She found it hard to walk a straight line. They carried the boy. And led her. Into the snow. Ankle high, knee high, hard enough to walk sober.

They dragged her when she tried to stop and rest.

"Solstice?" she asked.

"Solstice," they said, apparently the only English word they knew.

They walked for hours, past rock outcroppings and snowdrifts, to the top of the world.

When they finally stopped and offered her more strong chicha, she drank it gladly. At least it numbed the cold. Her uncovered fingers were stiffening, her toes complained of needles. Thousands of needles.

"How far?" she asked. She raised her palms and made the international sign of "where."

They pointed towards the summit. They were headed to the top, with no plan of return for her and Daniel. That was obvious. They were to be sacrificed. The girl in her dreams spoke true.

42 Chance to the rescue

Daybreak. Neither Maria nor Kalene had returned to the ruins. A single rifle shot in the night, that was all Randy and the rest had to think on. Just enough to bring to mind the ugliest of thoughts.

Isabel came over to Randy and Ed and the gang. "They're gone," she told them.

"The Shining Path?" said Randy.

"Yes."

"But what about Kalene? And Fernanda?"

"They don't have Fernanda," said Isabel. "They never did. As far as Kalene. I, I'm sorry to tell you, but Kalene is dead. That shot last night. My people found her body this morning."

"No!" shouted Chance.

Ed shook his bandaged head. "How terrible."

"*Que lastima*," said Paro.

"Do you know where Fernanda is?" asked Randy. "Is she in danger?"

"Yes, I fear so," said Isabel. "I, my people, they took her. Her and the boy. When they heard how special she was. For she is special. And the boy is special too. Especially to me."

"Took them?"

"For the solstice. I was wrong about the sacrifices. Old ways die hard in the Andes. I hesitated when they asked me for permission, the elders, and they misunderstood my hesitation as a yes. I screwed up, too preoccupied with the Shining Path I suppose. We were in such confusion. With the attack and all. Perhaps there is time for you to stop them."

"What the hell! Are you kidding me," Randy started to strike her, but Chance held him back. "Stop them from what?"

"My people will leave them to freeze on the mountain. Their souls for the Gods to take."

"You planned to fricking kill them!?"

"I didn't plan anything," said Isabel, her hawk face ugly with fatigue and tears. "Remember it was you who came to me. You who brought the boy. All the signs pointed to them as chosen ones. Paro said so."

"Because at that moment I was sure it was true," said Paro. "I question now why I was so sure. The herb perhaps misspoke."

"Oh yeah," said Chance. "Blame your drugs." He let Randy go and looked ready himself to pounce on Paro. "Can we stop the sacrifice?" asked Chance. "Can we save them?"

"Perhaps," said Isabel. "If you are fast, perhaps you can. They are several hours ahead."

"Why don't you send one of your runners to stop them?"

"I couldn't trust them to obey me," said Isabel. "Their belief in such things is stronger than their loyalty to me their leader."

"I'll help them," said Paro. "I'll guide them."

"Please," said Isabel. "We must put an end to it."

Paro studied his leader. Nodded. "An end." He turned to Chance. "You are strong and fast, Chance. I can lead you to where the others are taking them, with help from my coca. We must set out at once, though. It's a long race."

"I'm coming too," said Randy.

"No," said Paro. "You will only slow us down."

"Give me your coca, and I will keep up. For God's sake, she's my wife."

They quickly made light packs with covers and food and

water. Started up the trail at a brisk pace. Towards the snowy summit. In a race against Time, against Death.

43 Fernanda is the sacrifice

The rattling of Fernanda's teeth finally stop. She notices a warm lining to the bed of snow where she lay, where the Wari left her, and decides to stay. Where she lay. To close her eyes and sleep. If only the sun would let her. How can the sun be so bright when setting? How can the air, so thin, be so brutally cold? She would close her eyes, sleep all afternoon, sleep all night. And in the morning, she would rise and climb down off the mountain. In the morning she would get up.

A feeling. A shadow presence. She opens her eyes, expecting nothing, but in the dying sunlight before her stands a plump brown girl, her black hair cut in the Inca style. She is dressed in fine, colorfully dyed vicuna wool, and has a gold bracelet on her arm. Her large black eyes do not reflect the sun. The girl motions for Fernanda to get up, to follow her. Fernanda reaches but cannot grasp her hand. She rolls over, gets on all fours, her hands numb to the cold snow. She pushes herself to her feet. She stumbles, falls, rises again, staggers after the plump brightly dressed girl who is starting down the mountain.

"Are you the one that wants to sacrifice me? The one from my dreams?" She asks in English then Spanish.

The girl stops, turns. The wind whips up the snow, a great swirl envelopes the two of them.

"Who are you?" Fernanda asks, wiping ice crystals from her eyes.

The girl walks back up to where Fernanda was left to die, a sacrifice to the sun god Inti. Fernanda follows. The girl points to a snow-covered lump.

Fernanda kneels. Uses her arms to wipe snow from the lump, fearing what she will find. Perhaps she will find her own body curled in a fetal position, experiencing the final hallucinations that precede death by freezing. She breaks away a crust of ice around the body, noticing the bruised color of her own hands, the deep cracks in the skin of her fingers. She discovers dyed cloth and skin like a turkey's, plucked and frozen. She dislodges more snow, uncovering a dark plump face, a deep frozen, mummified face, with large eyes long frozen shut. Fernanda pulls back with a start. She recognizes this frozen lump of Incan girl. She is the same girl standing next to Fernanda, the same one waiting to show her the way.

Fernanda stands. Looks. The girl is gone. Fernanda realizes

she must have been hallucinating. Yet not hallucinating. Or still hallucinating. The boy, which of these lumps in the snow is the boy? Where is Daniel?

44 The last lap

"I can't keep up," yelled Randy. "You were right. How much farther?"

Paro tapped Chance on the shoulder. Pointed back to Randy, twenty yards down the trail.

They waited for him.

"I can't keep up," he repeated.

"I am fading myself," said Paro. They looked at each other. They wouldn't give up, but if they were too slow to arrive?

"I feel strong," said Chance. "I could run this mountain ten times. Helps to work in a mine."

"Then go on," said Paro. "Run in their snowprints. Get there before Fernanda and the boy freeze."

Chance took off without another word, running with the wind at his back, up the mountain, Kalene's voice in his head telling him that he could do it. That she loved him so for trying.

45 The finish line

He met them on their way down, not a half hour later. Five Wari men. The confused look on their faces! They barely tried to stop him as he plowed past. He did not like that. Wouldn't they have put up a bigger fight if they thought he could save Daniel and Fernanda?

Did it mean she was already dead? His ex-wife, Fernanda, the woman he still loved even though he knew he never deserved to have her in the first place.

The snow slowed him. Made his legs feel twenty pounds heavier. Somehow he kept up the pace. With the wind at his back and the coca leaves Paro had given him in his cheek, he felt he could make it. He knew he could make it. She wasn't dead yet. Only, only, the sun was going down. How would he see the snowprints in the dark?

46 Snowblind

Fernanda found the boy. Found Daniel half covered in the snow. She put her cold hand before his nose and could feel the hot exhalations. He was still alive. Could she carry him? Had no choice.

The sun slipped over the mountain peak just as she hauled the boy onto her back, fireman style.

She weaved a bit, found her footing. No good to fall. She might not be able to get up.

God help me, she said, though not sure which God she was addressing. Any that will listen, she supposed.

Darkness fell on her as she stagger-stepped down the slope. And with the darkness came a sense of doom.

How could she manage in the dark? Walk blindly down the mountain, off a cliff?

But not to worry. Her prayer was answered. The biggest moon she had ever seen sneaked its shiny head above the peaks, climbed into the starry sky, mounting her majestic thrown.

Fernanda could see. Almost better than with the sun, whose overpowering light had reflected off the snow, practically blinding her. The moon's light reflected off the snow like the shine off a baby's bottom.

She staggered. No, mustn't go down. Too heavy for her, the boy. So tired. So cold. The full moon brought light but no warmth. She gulped the frozen moon-lit air, which burst from her shocked lungs in great white plumes. She stopped. Couldn't go another step with such a load. She'd have to let the boy down, if she was going to survive the night. How could she do that? She couldn't just leave him to freeze. Maybe they could huddle together in the snow? Somehow get through the night that way, stealing each other's warmth? Her instinct told her no, she must push on. Must push on to the hut where they'd stayed the night before, to the hard bed and too short blanket. She forced herself to focus on that goal, to take a step forward. Another. And another. She staggered her way down with the boy on her shoulder, following the prints in the snow, the hated longed-for blanket practically before her eyes. Not such a long way to go, she told herself. Not such a long way down.

"Hello!" she heard the faraway call. She raised her eyes, scouted the snow before her.

"Yello," she tried to answer but managed only the sound of thin ice cracking and a wisp of steam.

Then she saw him. A tiny figure down the trail, marching through the snow like a windup doll.

Chance.

Dear Chance.

He's saved me.

47 Celebration

They gathered on the balcony of their favorite hotel in Cuzco, the one a short walk from the Plaza de Armas. Daniel's parents brought him to the join in the celebration with Ed, Randy, Fernanda, and Chance. Under a starry sky, the adults raised a glass of chicha to toast their fallen comrade, crazy Kalene, who had thought to take on the Shining Path all by herself.

"I still can't believe we found him," said Ed, watching Daniel cling to his mother. The black eye patch Ed wore made him look like a romantic pirate.

"I was a *soldado*," said Daniel.

"Yes you were," said Chance. "A right good soldier."

"So much we owe to you Randy," said Daniel's father, Pani, raising his glass. "We thank you from the bottom of our hearts for taking the case." Randy just smiled.

"And Chance," said Ed, "Thanks to Chance for taking a

detour. And running up a fricking mountain."

"Anytime," said Chance.

"You're not to tell a single person about this," said Randy. "That I helped you find your son. Remember. I could lose my job."

"We won't tell a soul."

Postword

In the study of the log house in the Arkansas woods, looking out the window on sparkling broken boulders from the quartz crystal mine he part owned with his wife Fernanda and his old pal Chance, Randy closed his email and opened the envelope with the Russian postmark.

"Word's out now," called Randy to Fernanda who was busy making a Mexican *sopita* in the kitchen. "I think someone in Peru blabbed cause I'm getting even more offers from all over the world. Everyone wants IBM's 007, IBM's Superman."

Fernanda came into the study, her breasts enlarged, her stomach showing.

"I like how you look, pregnant," said Randy.

"Wait a few months when I'm big as a horse."

"I'll like you even more!"

"What does Ed say?"

Randy perused the letter.

"He says he's grown accustomed to the glass eye. And while birdwatching in Siberia he met a woman. Marina. She is teaching him perspective."

"Imagine that!" said Fernanda. "Good for him."

She came over and sat on top of his desk. "You need to write back. Tell him that Chance reconnected with Maria. That her fool's gold is the top seller in our rock shop. She sent a bucket of quarter inch crystals last week, perfect for love charms. Too bad about her father, though."

"What do you mean, too bad? The bastard killed your friend."

"Yes. You're right. Strange how she slips my mind. Kalene. She was so brave to go to the Shining Path in search of me."

They both took a deep breath.

"So where to next? They want me in Brazil, Morocco, in France. Thailand, Cambodia, the Philippines?"

"After the child is born," she told him. "After you are a father, we'll throw a dart at the map on the wall."

And so they did.

ELSE

By Else

The First Kiss Mysteries

Bathing with the Dead

Her Heart in Ruins

All that we touch

Our Only Chance (available 2017)

More to come ...

Short Stories

First Kiss - Galley Beggar Press

Surviving on Mexican Shade — BBC (broadcast)

Also in the works

My Father's Lies

ELSE

About The Author

Software developer and dreamer of stories. Like most fiction writers, Ray Else's interest in writing began when he discovered books that talked to him, between the lines, books whose authors (spirits, invisible) sparked a conversation that the spirit in him responded to by writing stories himself. For other spirits. A daisy chain conversation.

Ray Else has a B.S. in Computer Science and an M.A. in Technical Instruction / Film History. He speaks English, Spanish and French. An American, he has lived in Mexico and France.

Job-wise he has loaded trucks for UPS, filled rat poison barrels on the night shift, digitized printed circuits, clerked at a department store, was a switcher for Channel 13 on the Texas border, installed inventory systems on oil rigs worldwide, and since 1995 has programmed for the likes of IBM and Rocket Software.

Married, with 4 grown kids and 11 grandkids, he enjoys traveling the world to visit friends and find new stories, occasionally rock-hounding – as shared on his website, rayelse.com.

You may contact Ray Else at rayelsemail@gmail.com.